THE PRISON DIALOGUE

A Transformative Work Of
Metaphysical Fiction

BY

RICHARD GAYZUR

To the Healing Embrace of Our Shared Universal Energy
Without Which This Book Could Not Have Been Imagined or Written.
And Especially to Archana and Owen.

You must be learning and feeling so many new things every day. And I want to hear about all of them. But for today, let me tell you some of the new things I am learning and feeling. Mirona, I have so many things to tell you.

RL1-05141964

THE PRISON DIALOGUE

OF RAUL AND MIRONA GUZMAN

EDITED WITH COMMENTARIES BY
MIRONA GUZMAN

ADDITIONAL COMMENTARIES BY

TERESA BETANCOURT   LYDIA FUENTES
DR. GINA GILFORD   BLAKE PALMER

PART I

1

How Buffy The Flamethrower Nearly Ended Our First Video Session

Mirona: (explodes) *Wait*!!

Blake wrote the *per*fect coda … *and*?! … all we need now is a *pre*face??! Are you in some … *fuck*ing … *pa*rallel *uni*verse!!? (storms off)

Gina: (gently) Mirona … Mirona? (lightly) You're just … mourning the loss of your relapse allotment (soft chuckle), OK? (silence) Mirona? (silence) Seriously, you're so close to …

Mirona: (spins back, hissing) *G*!ina … *Wha*!? … Why the *fuck* can't you … *e*!!!ver … j'st … (storms off)

2

2

EDITOR'S PREFACE

I was raised by a single mother when single motherhood raised eyebrows.[1] Otherwise, and due in no small part to my mother's perpetual efforts to paint us into the background, we [almost] lived like everyone else in that part of Chicago.

I never met my father. By the time I was birthed, Raul Guzman was already three months into a lifetime prison sentence. I suspected his existence, if not his residence, but couldn't confirm either until I was sixteen. After that, I devoted myself to hating him. And when that didn't work, to just forgetting about him. Gina describes my four decades of aggravated avoidance as half an inspired mutual choice.

Raul was convicted in December of 1958 for the murder of fashion photographer Miron [mee-*rown*] Podluski and the

---

1 Without attribution.

attempted murder of my mother. He committed neither crime [witnessed both, obviously], then promptly attempted suicide.

Somehow he was found guilty of both a premeditated murder and a felony murder. The ADA was taking no chances, and the judge seemed unfazed by the legal and logical conundrum posed by allowing his jury to convict him of two crimes with conflicting fact patterns. Beyond that, the transcript of my father's trial described a defense so abysmally inept it should have triggered an automatic mistrial [and probably would have if he hadn't been a 19-year-old Puerto Rican junkie]. The *New York Daily Mirror* labeled his jury's failure to impose the death penalty "*a blot on our criminal justice system.*"

Raul died at the Sing Sing Correctional Facility on December 8, 2016. From the get-go he'd been aware of the grounds for challenging his conviction, but chose never to pursue them. That choice appears to have been buttressed by what Gina describes as the energetic epiphany that took place during the sixth year of his incarceration, the night following my mother's only visit. She says that epiphany both liberated and inspired him to create the body of work excerpted in this book.

Beginning on May 14, 1964, my father wrote me one unmailed letter every day [except for two] for the remainder of his life—a total of 19,201 handwritten letters stuffed into three-ring binders that took up most of the free space in his cell. He also created one memorable YouTube video just four days before his death. I had no idea about any of these materials until a week after he died. It took me eighteen [especially intense] months to get through a large part of them.

Raul speaks to me as a little girl, then as a young woman, and then as an adult. I was surprised at how convincingly he could change his written voice to correlate with my age and my presumed experiences.

Gina doesn't think he was changing a thing. She says my father possessed an energetic knowledge of who I was and the things I was feeling at that moment. He was just writing to the daughter he encountered in his Soul. He also wrote as though he'd just read my response to his last letter. Somehow [and with no conscious participation on my part] we seemed to be carrying on a running dialogue replete with ponderings, revelations, and even the occasional disagreement.

To his endless credit, Raul didn't use his energetic skills to judge me or issue heavy-handed parental direction. Instead, the way Gina describes it, he was planting row after row of energetic kernels in my subconscious, one of which might suddenly germinate as I read a letter. She says those germinations have helped me access memories and feelings associated with the things that were happening in my life at the time and at a level of detail I couldn't have recalled any other way. My memories tend to dovetail with her explorations of my Soul and add another dimension to my chronic healing process.

This book is another one of those dimensions. It's been written [only] with Gina's constant encouragement and subject to her one mandate: that it fully honor the events and feelings of my life. As a practical matter, that's demanded some witheringly brutal honesty [even for Buffy The Flamethrower (minus most of her baffles and filters)].

Given the recent controversy surrounding Gina's show and my association with it, it's no surprise the media are revisiting the things my family experienced at Raul's burial. One esteemed televangelist likened [his misinterpretation of] those experiences to the Pentecostal experiences of Jesus's disciples. He then confirmed the limits of his biblical scholarship by likening me to the "tax collector" Saul, an apparent blunt-force assessment of my prior life as an investment banker, and declared it my sacred duty to become no less a defender of [his misinterpretation of] Christianity. God, he assured me, had designated his ministry my base of operations.

I declined his invitation on an episode of *Energy With Doctor Gina,* saying I could never be affiliated with a religious enterprise [and especially not one of his]. Doctor Gilford deftly reimagined my broadside as, "Our collective Energy is one with the Infinite Transcendence, the Loving Oneness, beyond all books, institutions, and theologies. It is at the heart and root of every major religion but not constrained by any one sectarian narrative or set of rules." Neither of our assertions sat especially well with the esteemed televangelist (currently spearheading a campaign that casts me as the "Archenemy of Christianity" and Gina as, well, quite possibly the Antichrist). [Ministry donations are up 147% year-over-year.]

I've never sought the demise of any religion. On the contrary, I agree with Gina that organized religion has been a key moral driver in the development of human civilization and an indispensable source of charitable works. Religions also have the unique potential to unify followers across denominational lines by promoting shared spirituality. These days they appear content with ushering followers into gated theological camps, each obsessed with defending the sectarian prerogatives of a God all camps claim to hold in common.

Rivalries aside, most of the American religious establishment now seems hell-bent on obliterating whatever might be left of the line between church and state. The most recent assaults involve NASA's historic discovery and almost immediate subsequent denial of sentient life in the internal ocean of Jupiter's moon Europa. The day before the second NASA news conference, the Southwest Evangelical Confraternity (SEC) issued a press release urging its members "and any rational person" to view the original NASA announcement with a healthy dose of skepticism. That same SEC release incorporated four sentences taken [word for word] from NASA's still-undelivered second announcement-retraction. The vitriol since spewed at NASA, the SEC, and the dysfunctional government in general continues to intensify even as more and more church organizations clamor to be recognized as "SEC Doctrine" adherents.

Sectarianism, overt or subtle, has been a distasteful part of human culture for millennia. States have long supported, allied, or flat out bedded down with religious bodies, recognizing that nothing motivates an army or transfers land, wealth, and power more efficiently than the overheard murmurings of a disgruntled God. We rail against the Islamists for their embrace of such a primitive strategy, especially in its most extreme forms, but we choose to ignore comparable behavior in the enlightened West. Consider: Four [civilized] nations are about to implement a series of "biblically sanctioned" social and military policies that would have been unthinkable in less fearful times. We seem to be harboring the belief that no matter how self-righteously antagonistic our behavior, we'll never reach the point of no return, whatever that point might be; or that it wouldn't be our fault if we ever got there; and even if we did get there, it's nothing a few more bombs and a few trillion dollars couldn't fix. For us.[2]

My father was a student of religion and history and was intensely aware of what was happening in the world. He understood that organized religion, for all its positive attributes, offered an unlikely solution to chronic hopelessness, which he described as the single greatest threat facing humanity. He recognized that

---

2 Whoever *us* winds up being.

even in an age of instant communication, people throughout the world, like many of the people he lived with, felt more alone and disconnected than at any time in human history.

What we must do, he urges in his letters, is rediscover and reembrace our one indistinguishable common denominator, our Universal Energy, which he describes as the positive, active, non-denominational interface that defines, links, and empowers all of us, connects us with all the matter and all the life that has ever been and will ever be, and remains the single most viable mechanism for inspiring the hope and compassion that must be shared by all mankind if we're to survive as a species.

These are the things my father intuited, then passed on to me. While I'm still exploring many of the personal implications, his teachings seem to make more practical sense than any other essential teachings I've come across. For that reason [and especially in light of very recent events], I've committed myself to disseminating knowledge of his writings and to working with Doctor Gilford to promote a broader understanding of Universal Energy and its applications through Energy Medicine.

What I've shared in this first book is only the smallest part of what my father created. Based on the many requests we've received, his entire output is being compiled into a series of annotated reference books that will be released periodically over the next six years. Several other projects involving Universal Energy and Energy Medicine are also in development.

I don't have memories of trips to the zoo or boring car rides or even classic shouting matches with my father. What I have instead is evidence of his innermost thoughts and feelings. That evidence includes one especially powerful letter describing a series of unimaginably painful events from his childhood, and it was clear from the even shakier handwriting that he was deeply affected by the memories. The more I read, the more I felt crushed by the emptiness. Suddenly I was off on another of my infamous rants, this one slathered in threats to cancel "every last *one* of these … *fuck*ing *pro*jects! … starting with this … fucking … *book*!!"

Gina was standing right next to me, seeing right through it all. At some point she was able to take my hand:

"What other life would you have chosen to live?"

[I've yet to respond.]

— *Mirona Guzman, New York City, March 2020*

3

Editor's Note

I've created a numbering system for Raul's letters and the other materials in this book. The system is straightforward and (for my purposes) effective. The first group of symbols on the upper left-hand side of a page (below the section name and number) identifies a letter by author and sequence. So RL1 would signify Raul's first letter, RL235 his two hundred thirty-fifth, and so on.

If the document is a commentary as opposed to one of the letters themselves, the letter C will follow the sequence designation. So RL3816C identifies a commentary on RL3816.

The second group of symbols indicates the eight-digit calendar date of the letter's composition.

A third group of symbols appears only with commentaries and identifies the author of the commentary and its sequence among other commentaries on that letter. So RL1C-05141964-TB2 translates as a commentary on letter RL1 which Raul composed on May 14, 1964. The commentary was written by TB (Teresa Betancourt) and is the second commentary on that letter. Note that I've also employed a few readily comprehensible variations on this basic system.

Five people have contributed commentaries for this book: Teresa Betancourt (TB), my mother; Lydia Fuentes (LF), my god-mother; Dr. Gina Gilford (GG), my doctor of Energy Medicine; Blake Palmer (BP), my daughter; and myself, Mirona Guzman (MG) [Roni Podluski in a prior life]. I suspect there'll be a number of additional commentators contributing to the anno-tated reference books as well as additional types of materials to be catalogued. I'll leave it to future editors to expand on the current system or to create a more efficient one.

Note that I am a compulsive editor, and that I detest the editing and revision tools provided with Word software. Accordingly, I've reduced my editing system for this book down to a series of [bracketed] words and phrases indicating (to me) that a partic-ular edit is no more than two editing cycles old. Gina has yet to decide if all evidence of my editing will be eliminated from what-ever she declares to be my final draft.

Finally, and for what it's worth, my first draft of this book was on track to easily exceed five hundred pages and include twenty-four of my father's letters as opposed to the present ten. Up to that point, Gina had expressed no opinion about its length.

When I raised the issue in the course of yet another unfettered bitching session, her response was, "Wouldn't it be wonderful to experience it as a single meditation?" I've never successfully meditated, much less written anything that could be mistaken for a meditation.

But I've done a hell of a lot of editing.

THE PRISON DIALOGUE

4

RAUL'S FIRST LETTER

(RL1-05141964)

Dear Mirona,
  I saw your picture yesterday. You were standing in front of your house. What a pretty little girl you are. And very smart, too, I am sure. Just like Mommy.

You must be learning and feeling so many new things every day. And I want to hear about all of them. But for today, let me tell you some of the new things I am learning and feeling. Mirona, I have so many things to tell you.

Where do I start? I know. First let me tell you something special about you and me. When I was five years old, just like you, I lived in a house with my mommy, just like you do. And I did not know who my real daddy was, just like you did not know until today.

Here is something I learned today. It is something I never really knew before. I learned that I love my daughter, my beautiful Mirona, very much. And that makes me very happy.

I will write to you again tomorrow.

I love you, sweetheart.

Besos,

Daddy

5

Editor's Commentary On Raul's First Letter

(RL1C-05141964-MG1)

No typeface can convey the graphic intensity in Raul's handwriting, especially in his early letters. As intelligent as he was [my father graduated top of his prison class], he still wrote in this cartoonish kind of script that usually overemphasized and sometimes skewed the obvious meaning of his words.

RL1 was written the day after Mom's only visit to Sing Sing, which she still describes as the most emotionally draining experience of her life. She says she was completely devastated by the sadness in his eyes as he gazed at my picture pressed against a thick glass panel. Those eyes grew even sadder when she revealed my name, just the slightest variation on that of her murdered fiancé.

My baptismal name, Mirona Andrea Podluski, was the linchpin of Mom's efforts to establish my legitimacy while somehow imagining she was hiding me from the assistant district attorney who'd threatened to take me away if she didn't conform her testimony to his version of the facts. The threat was an obvious bluff, but the fear stuck with her for decades. There was never a time I couldn't sense it.

Mom had already changed her own name legally from Teresa Maria Betancourt to Theresa Maria Podluski. With her fair skin, refined manners, and the fact that we lived in the most Polish neighborhood in Chicago, she could just about pull it off. I was always a visual question mark but not quite an outright disqualification.

I vaguely remember the bus ride from Chicago to New York. However, I have one especially strong memory from Aunt Lydia's place in the Castle Hill section of the Bronx while Mom made her cryptic trip to Sing Sing.

Lydia Fuentes, my godmother, isn't a blood relative. She's nine years Mom's senior and semi-adopted her in late 1957 when she and her parents moved from an upscale San Juan suburb to the building directly across from Aunt Lydia's on West 64th Street in Manhattan. Aunt Lydia had already semi-adopted my father while the two of them were living in the same San Juan shelter. She went on to semi-adopt my maternal grandparents after Mom moved us to Chicago.

My memory involves Aunt Lydia's living room. It was [and still is] more like a large storage closet or an uncurated museum. After they filmed *West Side Story*, while parts of West 64th Street and a few surrounding blocks were being demolished to make room for Lincoln Center, Aunt Lydia was busy collecting keepsakes of her ten years in the neighborhood. There were graffiti-covered bricks, tar-filled bottle caps, a "No Parking" sign still on the pole, and even one of those three-handled soda-jerk mechanisms from the candy store where she bought her Lucky Strikes.

And there were photos, piles of them, mostly the curly-edged black-and-white Kodak Brownie variety. One pile was topped off by a picture of a teenage boy and girl just at my five-year-old eye level. He was slouched on his stoop, staring. She was standing over him and looked like she'd just snapped her head to the camera as the picture was taken. It was my mother and father on West 64th Street in November of 1957. I remember picking up the picture and instantly recognizing him. Apparently no amount of isolation was going to keep Raul from attaching a face to that introductory letter.

I also remember having my first Silver Lady dream around that time, although I can't say for sure it was the night after Mom's visit, which would've made it the same night as [what Gina describes as] my father's epiphany.

In the dream, I'm floating in the air at night looking down at a dark river. A beautiful lady appears. She's floating just inches above the water and begins to glow with all these silvery lights.

As she drifts to a point directly below, her lights suddenly beam straight up and just splash all over me. They feel like soda bubbles feel on your nose, except now I can feel them all over my body.

Then I'm drifting upward and I realize I can do somersaults and pirouettes and fly as far as I want in any direction. The higher I fly, the more her lights start to feel like all these arms holding me, and I'm so happy I even start to laugh.

And *just* as I start to laugh [just at that exact second!], my Silver Lady looks up ... and she *smiles* at me.

— *Mirona Guzman*

6

My Mother's Commentary on Raul's First Letter

(RL1C-05141964-TB2)

I still find it hard to imagine one person could generate not only all the letters, but all the selfless love and caring that was poured into them, and sustain that effort in prison for more than five decades. I am privileged to have had Raul in my life and grateful to my daughter for the chance to add my comments to hers.

Mirona speaks of the fear I can now admit to carrying in my soul. I always associated the source of that fear with the events preceding Raul's trial, and especially with the actions of the assistant district attorney. He had developed not so much a theory of the case as a fictional story that suited his purpose. According to that story, Raul fired the bullets that killed Miron and could have killed me even as his friend, Benito, begged him not to go through with it.

I was sitting in Miron's car and clearly saw two shots fired from inside Benito Sanchez's car. Raul was standing outside both cars, so there was no possible way he could have fired them. Unfortunately, Mr. Sanchez and the car's other occupants were killed in a crash a few minutes later. Raul was the only person left to blame.

During my first pretrial meeting the ADA slowly walked me through his version of the facts in very simple English. When I disagreed with it, he became infuriated and screamed all manner of threats.

I screamed back, and then half expected him to hit me. Instead he slowly leaned over his desk, stared at my belly, and in the coldest voice I'd ever encountered asked, "Do you want to keep that souvenir from your junkie boyfriend?" I will never forget my reaction to those words. Thinking back, it made no sense that he could take Mirona from me either by a forced abortion or after she was born, but those were the fears that instantly overwhelmed me.

A few weeks later, I was one of five "eyewitnesses" testifying to the same false set of facts. From then on, my fear of that ADA was amplified by my guilt over supporting a farce that could have very well ended with Raul's execution.

I especially remember the look on the ADA's face when it became clear the jury could not reach a unanimous death penalty verdict. As the judge sentenced Raul to life imprisonment without parole, I felt the ADA's eyes settle on me. And I just knew he was going to take his anger out on my child. Anticipating this, I had already asked Miron's partner, Andrew, to help me move out of state. He and his friends responded with a job and my first apartment in Chicago. They understood far better than most the damage that could be done by a vengeful civil servant operating within a compliant system.

Miron Podluski was a very dear friend and a remarkably talented fashion photographer. (He took the photographs of me used in the Piaget ads displayed on the Times Square Tower in 2001.) I decided to accept his offer of marriage once it became apparent even my pregnancy would not stop Raul from using drugs. At the same time, Miron needed a visible spouse or risked being outed as a gay man which, in 1958, would have meant the end of his career. A show marriage appeared the best solution to both our problems.

Tragically, my very dear friend was murdered the day after he gave me an exquisite engagement ring. It had been his mother's, and I cherish it to this day.

Fear and shame nearly kept me from visiting Raul in prison. (Thank goodness for Lydia's not so gentle persistence!) I had this premonition our bus would be stopped at the New York border and armed agents would drag Mirona away. As it is, I made Lydia promise me Mirona would not so much as look out a window while I visited her father. Still, the Infinite Transcendence managed to facilitate an introduction between the two of them. Even as I wallowed in self-pity, Infinite Love kept flowing into our lives.

I expected my fears to subside after we returned to Chicago. Instead, they grew stronger and remained a driving force behind every major decision I made. Arguably, they helped fuel a successful business career that provided some advantages and imagined protections for Mirona but, sadly, little real peace for either of us.

When Mirona moved back to New York, the fears intensified again. As she completed her MBA and then landed job after successful job, there was never the slightest letup. As she became a public figure with countless articles written about her, even when she was made chief operating officer at Morgan Stanley, I still envisioned that ADA walking into her office one day and just whisking her off, the fear was so deeply etched into my soul.

I will never be able to adequately express my gratitude to Gina for the work she has done with me. During my first visit to her as a doctor of Energy Medicine, she identified my fears, not as the product of my experiences with that ADA but as a negative energetic frequency that had been passed on to my father and then on to me, only to be further magnified by the events of the trial.

My father had spent his entire married life guarding what he had been told were unspeakable secrets about my mother. She was a descendant of one of the earliest Spanish families in San Juan, but that did not spare her from rape at the hands of a pedophile uncle when she was nine.

Her trauma was only surpassed by her family's shame. Of course, they dealt with it as any such family would have dealt with it in 1927 Puerto Rico: My great-uncle was shipped back to Spain and my increasingly hysterical mother was removed to a sanitarium where, it was hoped, she would eventually forget what had happened to her.

Guarding my mother's past had the unfortunate effect of reviving my father's own childhood traumas and associated negative frequencies: His father had abandoned him and his mother when he was only six. Yet he became—improbably in those days—a successful businessman and rose to the level of executive vice president at the largest business document translation company in Latin America. His resulting financial status made him at least a marginal suitor for my mother. (That, and the fact that she had no other serious suitors. Rumors concerning her unfortunate past had always circulated.)

They met at a charity event sponsored by my father's company. To hear him describe it at my mother's wake, her devastating outward beauty was only eclipsed by the sadness he sensed within. At that moment, without realizing it, he had committed himself to protecting unborn me from the knowledge he would soon be sworn never to reveal by my mother's similarly sworn but very talkative older sister. I was never allowed to meet her and have only fleeting childhood memories of my other maternal and paternal relatives.

My father's protections involved ceaseless efforts to portray my mother's deteriorating mental state as anything but what and why it really was. Those efforts frightened and infuriated me. I felt like a stranger in my own home and acted out my pain and fear with little regard for his or hers. My Soul had inherited two generations of a negative frequency, and I was about to add a third fortified with my own variations on hiding and protecting before passing it all on to my daughter.

This is what made Gina's work so amazing. Within two sessions she and I had drained more than ninety percent of those negative frequencies from my Soul. I was left with a lightness and a sense of release and relief I never imagined possible.

But that was only the beginning. We have continued to work on preserving my energetic integrity. She has helped me develop a series of spiritual exercises and meditations I try to repeat every day and that have made my time with my daughter, my granddaughter, and Lydia a source of ever-increasing joy.

Occasionally I allow myself to imagine how much better my life might have been if I had known everything about my mother and father, or what Raul was doing in prison, or if Gina had come into our lives sooner. I know these are useless and even destructive thoughts. Left unchecked, they can drive me to reconstruct the same self-pity frequency and the desire for unachievable control that left me hopeless and separated from my family in the first place.

I am also very pleased to be co-sponsoring a series of women's empowerment seminars focusing on not-for-profit career strategies and pathways to energetic integrity. As my Raul describes it in his Corollary to the First Rule, I am *"passing on the good things that were passed on to me."*

That is true empowerment.

— *Teresa Betancourt*

7

EDITOR'S NOTE

Although Aunt Lydia's comments don't relate specifically to ARL1 or any one of Raul's letters, I think it's important to introduce her here. Without Lydia Fuentes and her lifelong dedication to my mother and father, none of these letters would exist. Raul would've died in San Juan long before he and Mom ever met and, of course, I wouldn't have been born. Gina says we're living through the results of a time-inverted choice made on a universal level at some point in the future. I'm not so sure I can accept the idea of inverted time, but I imagine things work out as well as they can.

While Aunt Lydia was thrilled to learn her memories would be included in this book, she insisted they be presented exactly as she recalled them—which meant word for word in her inimitable vocal style with full visual descriptions. To see/hear her explain it during our first video session: "If people gonna unnerstan' whod hoppeen ... dey gotta understan', ya know... (taps her chest) dees! No way you ca' make dees shit soun' too pretty, ya know? Like ... ya know, like ... de way you makin' you'self soun' een de bouk! (chuckles) OK, Mirona? Heh?"

That's my Aunt Lydia—every wrinkled, unedited, irresistible morsel of her. My original plan was to record maybe three or four total hours of conversation about her life in Puerto Rico, her time with my parents in New York City during 1957 and 1958, and then whatever else she cared to add.

Our first session started at around noon and ended at one in the morning. Two other highly productive, Corona Light–lubricated, full-ashtray sessions followed shortly [our audio engineer finally gave up trying to modify her behavior]. In total we recorded nearly twenty-three hours of Aunt Lydia's memories and life commentaries. It all ended late one afternoon with a long silence. She finally slapped a hand on the table and declared, "Yeah, das eet." (long pause) "You gonna make dees a movie, too ... right?" (collective laughter)

Aunt Lydia identified five segments she wanted included in this book [including a snippet of my pre-preface meltdown, barely the appetizer for an epic rant that nearly ended our first session]. I finally convinced her to let me transcribe them into a reasonably comprehensible form of English, toning down most of her color- ful pronunciations but preserving most of her cadence and man-

nerisms. And, yes, we're exploring the production of a full-length movie based on her life.

The transcripts that follow include several speakers besides Aunt Lydia and me: Teresa Betancourt [my mother recently changed her name back legally], Dr. Gina Gilford, Blake Palmer [my now 22-year-old daughter], Jason our [referee] videographer, and one very nervous audio engineer [no one remembers his name]. The Greek chorus of background laughers consists mostly of technician types from other studios in the building who just had to drop by when they heard what we were attempting. Aunt Lydia welcomed one and all.

8

Aunt Lydia's Video Commentaries on Everything—Part 1

(RL1C-05141964-LF3-1)

Audio Engineer: Testing, one, two ... On mike two, please?

Mirona: Testing, one, two. Testing. Is that ...?

Jason: Yeah, that's good. OK. We're rolling.

Lydia: (in the distance) *How* long they been in? ... (unintelligible) Heh? ... Whaddaya think, I'm from *Eng*land or somethin'? (laughter) This how the *Queen* gotta drink it? (footsteps approaching, chair moving, laughter fades)

Audio Engineer: (anxiously) I'm sorry! Could you ... keep that beer away from the ...

Lydia: Hey, *relax!* (nose to mike, red-zoning) We gonna *be* here for a while, you know? (looks about, off mike) Mirona, where's the *cenicero* (ashtray)?

(*five minutes later*)

Mirona: Aunt Lydia, tell me about your parents.

Lydia: My mother's name was *Inez Cruz.* She was a whore, you know, at the house that, uh … that my father made into the school … later. (long pause) Mirona, look, I'm gonna *say* all this, OK? I ain't holdin' *noth*in' back. I mean … I don't plan on *dy*in' with this shit … (taps chest)

Mirona: No, say exactly … whatever you like.

Lydia: Good … *Good!* (lights cigarette) OK! … Now … My father was the mon*sig*nor. Monsignor Arturo Fuentes. *Beauty*ful man. From *España* (Spain). He had the green eyes, like me. (scoffs, gestures) Well! … Maybe not … you know …

Mirona: Wait … a monsignor? A *priest?* … How'd *that* happen?

Lydia: (stares, with *barrio* swagger) How duh fuck you *think?* (peals of laughter)

Mirona: That's not … (pause) You think by *now* I'd … (laughter fades)

Lydia: Look. I seen *ev'*rything in that house. And my father, he told me once, he didn't really *wan*na be a priest but … you know … his *fam*ily. Big shots. In *Spain!* First son gotta be a *priest,* you know?

But he was a *good* priest … and a *good* father! (chuckles) Don't know how he done it. 'Specially then. You know, had to be a secret. Me and him … and Sister Paolo. She know about the, uh … She run the, uh … the *shel*ter where I live … after me and my mother get kicked outta the house … by the pimp. Same guy who kill her … and my father. Same time. (pause, remembers) And *Jesús* (Hay-*zeus*)!

Mirona: Who was Jesús?

Lydia: (scoffs) Jesús! When my mother was *real*ly high? She think he was her *boy*friend! He was just some … some *push*er … doin' her, sellin' *heroína* (heroin) … all kinna cheap *drogas* (drugs). Work for these two, uh … these, uh … (speaks *in Spanish,* off mike.)

Teresa: (off mike) He was a drug retailer for two suppliers. They were working for one of the big San Juan cartels. In the early forties.

Lydia: Yeah. And my mother was livin' with him, doin' it with his, uh … sou-*pli*-uz! … so he get his drugs a little cheaper, you know? (pause) He was just *usin'* her.

Mirona: So … how'd Raul come into the picture?

Lydia: OK … (deep breath) Well … They was this *real*ly pretty girl … *Celia* … *mulata* (Latina of apparent African descent). Workin' in the house with my mother. Jesús done *her* … even when he was doin' my *moth*er. And she had his *ba*by. That was Raul.

And I know, 'cause I can see the *lights,* Jesús gonna be a *real* problem for that little boy. So I make a promise. (shakes finger) Nothin' … *No*body gonna hurt Raul! 'Specially Jesús. I take care of him all the time … even back in the school. (shift) Even that night, when everybody get *kill*! (elevates) Even the *pimp*! 'Cause the sou-*pli*-uhs shoot *him* after … (shrugs, softly) after he shoot my mother … and Jesús … then my father.

(pause, re-elevates) The house where Jesús was *livin*' in? Was on *fire*! And … and I go in and I find Raul just … *standin*' there! (shift) And the guy who shoot the pimp? I *seen* him! And he seen *me*! So next day, I just … I leave Raul with Celia. (head shake) She wasn't doin' so good. And I come here. (pause, looks off) I was … sixteen. (silence, knocking on a distant door)

Gina: (off mike) That's Blake. (calls out) Come in! (door opens, closes)

Blake: (off mike) Thanks … (approaching footsteps, kisses) Hi, Grandma … Hi … (unintelligible) Hey, Aunty Lyd! … Hi … Hi, Mom …

Mirona: Hey, Beebs. (kisses)

Gina: I asked Blake to come during lunch and listen and maybe give Matthew some ideas for a new segment. (to Blake) How's your second week?

Blake: He's brilliant! I love working for Matthew … well … for you, Aunt Gina.

Gina: (kindly) He is. And he thinks highly of you, too.

Blake: (chuckles, pause) I'm sorry. Did I interrupt …?

Lydia: Nah, dat's OK! I always love to see my *Blakita*. (to Teresa) Is like lookin' a' *you* when you was a kid! (to Blake) You wanna *cerveza* (beer), baby? They still nice and *warm*!

Blake: (insider's chuckle, mimicking) Nah, dat's OK!

Mirona: (slight edge) You were talking about the lights.

Lydia: Heh … the lights. Seen 'em my whole life since I'm … I dunno, like … *three* years old? … (to Teresa) except for a little time before you come to Sixty-four' Street. They *help* me … you know … what people *feel*in'. And sometime what they gonna *do*. Like the guy almost kill my mother in the house that time. Uhm!

Mirona: Do you actually see … *lights*?

Lydia: (sighs) Is not like … OK, is … (gestures, points to ceiling lights) Is not like *these* … but … (tongue click, multiple gestures, shift) Gina, you splain to them. C'mere.

Gina: (off mike) Lydia, this is about you. Just say it the way you …

Lydia: (over her) No, no, no, no … No, c'mere. I like the way you say it. (unintelligible) I said, c'mere! … Gina? (tongue click, off mike) C'*mere*!! (chair moves)

Gina: (on mike) Lydia's talking about Universal Energy. The same … force … the *stuff* that's been around since before the beginning of our time and that binds, defines, and empowers everyone and everything. The people who can sense it experience it in different ways. Some refer to it as "the lights." However it's described, Energy is experienced as a kind of … *vis*ion, but one that's beyond our traditional senses. (Lydia hand-signals "continue.")

Now … people with the vision can experience it at different times in their lives. Sometimes, when the vision is dormant, people can be trained to activate their … their *gift*. And sometimes the gift just activates on its own, at some special moment. That seems to be what happened with Raul. And sometimes the gift can just go dark … for days or even years. (fondly) And then there's a small group of people who are just born with the lights on. Like Lydia.

Lydia: (off mike) You too, Gina.

Gina: (chuckles) Lydia used to babysit for me on the West Side when my mother was at work. (to Lydia) I must have been, what? … about six? (unintelligible) Even then, if I tried, I could recognize different Energy patterns. But I never said anything because I was afraid people would think I was crazy. And for some reason I just … I knew I could tell Lydia. She validated everything I was feeling … and seeing. It was the first time I … (pause, points, smiles, choking up) My *God!* It was *you* … that … that *moment* … when I had the chance to study Energy and, and then develop the Energy Medicine model I, I just … I *jumped* at it! Lydia, if it wasn't for *you* … *then!* … I don't know what …

Lydia: (off mike, lightly, over her) OK, OK. Dat's it, Gina. C'mon. *Time's* up! Le's go. (light laughter, chairs move, on mike) Hey, one more word, you don' watch *King Kong* on TV tonight! (snaps fingers, points) Eight feet away, OK? (more laughter)

Gina: (girlishly) You remember? (laughter fades, chair moves)

Mirona: When was the first time you met Mom?

Lydia: (on mike, to Teresa) You know. I told you. I was graduatin' from eight' grade. At the, uh, the *big* school, the *real* school,

Santo Rosario (Holy Rosary) … next to the *big* church. My father give me my diploma and he say this *really* nice speech. And then they give these, uh … *med*als … to the little kids. The *smart* ones. Teresa, you was in … what?

Teresa: (off mike) I was in first grade.

Lydia: Yeah. And when you come walkin' right in fronna me, all of a sudden I seen the lights … from *you*! They wasn't … the same like Raul, but I knew. They was suppose to go to*geth*er, you know? And … and I *knew*! I'm suppose to *do* something … with you and me … and Raul. (pause, smile) I just knew.

9

▥

Raul's Second Letter

(RL2-05151964)

Dear Mirona,

Did you sleep well last night? Did you stay asleep the whole night and not wake up, even once? Yes, that is the same thing that happened to me. And I did not have any scary dreams. I almost always have them. Instead, last night, I had a very happy dream. It is so nice to have dreams like that, isn't it?

I have to get ready for school now. I go to a special school where I live and I have to study for a test today. I want to get a very good grade.

You must be thinking about kindergarten in September. I know you will do very well. Mirona, I am so proud of you.

I will write to you again tomorrow.

I love you, sweetheart.
Besos,
Daddy

10

EDITOR'S COMMENTARY ON RAUL'S SECOND LETTER

(RL2C-05151964-MG1)

My mother doesn't remember telling Raul anything about my starting kindergarten. She does remember I stopped my bed-wetting around then. Gina says my father wasn't just encountering me energetically but also clearing out some of the simpler negative frequencies he found. She calls it a kind of "spontaneous surrogacy."

For some reason every time I read his second letter and others from this period I can imagine Raul's accented voice blending with Fred Rogers's nasal twang. I remember, at the time I was addicted to *Father Knows Best*. There he was, pitch-perfect Robert Young, his all-American family, and one happy ending after the next. The show captivated and saddened me at the same time.

Then Fred Rogers came along. He didn't try to fix things. Fred and his puppets just validated the things kids felt, including my sadness. The minute I laid eyes on him, I knew my Robert Young affair was over.

Fred Rogers didn't do his first episode of *Mr. Rogers' Neighborhood* until about four years after Raul wrote his first letter, but Gina's positive my Soul was experiencing Fred's show in previews the whole time. I was also a nine-year-old by then, and rapidly aging out of Fred's target audience. The thing is, no one, not even the people who thought they really knew me [even my mother didn't know this until recently], realized I was a closet Fred Rogers fan right through high school.

The first time I appeared on Gina's show we spent the better part of the hour discussing my father's early writings. Some contrarian audience member couldn't imagine how it was possible I hadn't been "cured for *life*!" after experiencing hundreds of Raul's surrogacy sessions, "and at such an *early age*!"

My first reaction was the emptiness. I think Gina sensed it, and she jumped in with one of her typically brilliant responses. She said we've all been conditioned by the media to believe energetic events produce plenary and permanent changes. And while that notion makes for big box offices, it has almost nothing to do with reality.

She used the analogy of a runner's damaged knee. Once repaired by a skilled physician, the knee can be used again, but only after a period of healing, rehabilitation, and continuing efforts to avoid reinjuring it.

Gina called Raul my skilled physician. He could do his best to repair my spiritual knee, check for infection, and tend the wound site. But he couldn't prevent all the other damage my Soul was experiencing. His letters seem to recognize that.

Rather than trying to undo all that damage, she believes Raul was creating a kind of energetic owner's manual for my life. Like every other owner's manual I've ever ignored, I'd never read this one in advance, but there it was when I really needed it.

Without my father's thankless efforts, I'm guessing I would've found a way to crash and burn ages ago. Even if my life wound up anything like what it's been, some formulaic *New York Times* obituary would have already announced my departure. I'm just guessing.

Instead, for some reason, I get to stick around and introduce the world to Raul's writings.

[While Gina keeps trying to wedge them into my Soul.]

— *Mirona Guzman*

11

RAUL'S 1,320TH LETTER

(RL1320-12251967)

Dear Mirona,

Merry Christmas, sweetheart.

I hope you receive wonderful presents and get to spend time with Mom and the people who mean a lot to you. That is the most important part, being with the people you care about.

My students (I have thirty-five now) have been very generous to me this year. As I mentioned yesterday, I have been receiving some very nice cards and the type of gifts people here give one another. I have also received letters from three of their parents thanking me for teaching their children to read and write for the first time. Imagine that. Grown men who never learned to read or write. All of them went to school at least as long as you have. Can you imagine anyone going to school that long and still not being able to read and write?

There are things I see here that make me wonder how people become the way they do. The people I live with are different from one another in many ways. But I cannot help thinking there is something very important they all have in common, something more than where they grew up or who their friends were or how much money they had to spend or how well they did in school. Let me think about it some more.

I have a history student named Desmond. His parents moved to New York City from the island of Jamaica when he was only two. They worked very hard and bought a small house in a nice neighborhood. Desmond did well in school until the sixth grade. Then, the way he explains it, his anger took over. He says it was always there, but he was able to keep it under control.

One day he brought a knife to school. His plan was to hurt several students and teachers during recess, but the knife accidentally fell out of his pocket during class and his teacher sent him to the principal's office.

Naturally, the principal wanted to know why he had a knife. Desmond said he wanted to hurt people. The principal asked why. Desmond did not have an answer. He felt angry and confused. The confusion made him even angrier. He says that is the day he chose to be bad. But I am not sure he chose anything. What do you think? Have you ever just felt angry and confused and did not know why? I know I have.

The first day Desmond was in my class, he refused to call me "teacher" or "Raul" like my other students. Instead, he pointed at the scars on my cheek and said, "I'm going to call you Cheek-o." He said it in an angry way. Several of my students started to laugh. Suddenly, I had the same feelings I used to have when I was young. I felt angry and confused and, for a minute, I thought I was going to lose control. But for some reason I did not. I just let a few seconds go by. Then I touched my cheek and said, "You know what? That was pretty good. You can call me Cheek-o if you like." That was the end of it. I felt better and the class went on as usual.

Desmond still calls me Cheek-o sometimes, but never in an angry or a mean way. Yes, he still feels anger, but I think he is getting better. He even gave me a Christmas card.

Have a very beautiful Christmas, Mirona.

I will write again tomorrow.

I love you, sweetheart.

Besos,

Daddy

12

EDITOR'S COMMENTARY ON RAUL'S 1,320TH LETTER

(RL1320C-12251967-MG1)

I found this enlarged printout of a black-and-white Polaroid taken on Christmas Day, 1967. We're in our upstairs apartment at Uncle Peter's house in Chicago. Mom and me are sitting on the floor in front of this perfectly shaped, elegantly incandescent balsam fir. I'm wearing a bulky white turtleneck sweater, tailored camel pants, a shearling vest and matching boots, and the biggest scowl on earth. She's as effortlessly elegant as the tree, this time in her velvet burgundy bell-bottoms and that iridescent white silk blouse.

I remember, when I looked at that Polaroid the first time, all I could see was all that white and light making my face look darker than I already knew it was. I bolted into my bedroom, tore off my clothes, scribbled on the sweater and the vest with a ballpoint, and reappeared just long enough to scream to all present that I would "*Never!*" wear a stitch of that outfit again. Mom must have spent a small fortune on it. If she hadn't hidden that Polaroid, I swear [with all the anger and confusion], I would've definitely ripped it up.

By then I was totally convinced my skin color was the first [and only] thing people saw and the last thing they thought they needed to see. Of course, just to make things worse, there was the name. I mean, what kind of an idiotic name was "Mirona Andrea Podluski"? OK, maybe Podluski could've been an adoption artifact.

But "Mirona"? New teachers usually came up with *my*-runna. That was the giveaway they were fans of Myron Floren from *The Lawrence Welk Show*, or some borscht belt comedian named Myron Cohen who could even make farty old Ed Sullivan crack up.

And if the Old Country pronunciation—mee-*rown*—wasn't weird enough, there was always that final "a" terminating the unpronounceable mee-*rown*-uh as it Latinized some dead Slav's name. Mom said it was a common practice.

Her fair skin, an S-K-I surname, and [just a hint of] an undifferentiated accent meant Missus Theresa Maria Podluski presented as a passable Polack in our little Diversey enclave. The thing is, I'd already figured out she was a Puerto Rican. But why even bring it up? Only *White* people came from Puerto Rico, right? And I wasn't White. So the only logical conclusion was I'd been fathered by the world's darkest Pole.

And I actually embraced that absurd thesis right through the end of second grade. Mom reinforced it with this dulcet mantra memorializing Polish immigrant fashion photographer Miron Andrej Podluski, her late husband and my biological father, as "*a very kind man*" who'd been killed in a New York City traffic accident in July of 1958 just four weeks after their wedding. When I began demanding a more rational explanation for my complexion [after confirming the other three colored kids in my school were <u>definitely</u> not Polish] Mom started in with her Puerto-Rico-is-the-great-melting-pot deflection, which gave me nothing I could comprehend or use. And I needed a convincing plot line to explain my existence.

For a while I came up with Harry Belafonte. He was almost a full shade darker than me and secretly adored by every White girl on the planet. Early in third grade I rechristened him a second cousin on my father's side and allowed the rumor to circulate that it was a disquieting bit of family history I preferred not to discuss.

By then I realized I could outslap any girl in my class—which made me feared but not necessarily respected. [The little turds still made fun behind my back.] My scholastic career would be reduced to nothing more than a marathon bitch-slap unless I could find a better way to herd cats.

I also realized I was much smarter than anyone else in my class, including my teacher. Now I discovered what my brain and my mouth could do as an integrated weapons system.

Poor little Althea Johnson was the shortest girl in third grade and black as night. She never said two words, hid in plain sight, and as the designated "lesser-than" quietly gave everybody's ego a little boost. Althea would be my first of countless victims. I had absolutely no reason to attack her but, somehow, I just knew I had to do it.

One day in the schoolyard during a game of hopscotch, Althea passed by a little too close. I froze, mid-hop, and in my current version of superior English asked something like, "How long did it take to row the slave boat from Africa?" There was this extended silence, then the complicit peals of high-pitched giggles. Third-grade insecurities were momentarily shrouded [except for Althea's]. I didn't feel even a tingle of remorse when she teared up and slinked off. Before Sister Mary Consolata could pound out her Sonata For Solo Class Bell, I'd deputized my first all-White posse.

Jennifer Pollizzi looked at least as tough as her name. We'd never actually had it out but I always had this feeling she could be a major problem. The Big Po was definitely there the first time I skewered Althea and must have seen me pull off any number of similar attacks.

She caught me completely off guard with an invitation to her house later that Christmas Day together with three girls who'd never been posse members. We were supposedly going to listen to her new copy of *Magical Mystery Tour*. It was an obvious setup, and I was nervous about going but I knew I'd look like a total wimp if I backed out.

Mom was in the living room with Uncle Peter and Uncle Andrew when I got off the phone and announced my departure. After the usual give and take, she made the unforgiveable error of asking, "Mirona, when do you think you'll return?"

It was the name. She'd gotten it *horribly* wrong. I'd just spent weeks training everyone I knew to call me Roni, and I did not suffer backsliders kindly. My brain-mouth reflexively shot back something bitchy-imperious like, "You will call me *Roni*!" And all that earned me was "the look," the most benign weapon in her sparse arsenal.

Jennifer lived upstairs in another two-family home about three blocks away. Her place was smaller than ours and stuffed to the rafters that day with loud, laughing relatives, most shouting what could have been Sicilian or maybe Neapolitan. [My first whiff of perfected Southern Italian cooking was equally disorienting.]

We wedged ourselves into Jennifer's tiny bedroom and started listening. Midway through "I Am The Walrus" she lifted the needle, glared at me for all eternity, and finally said, "How come you keep picking on Althea?" As the shock wore off, I mustered up my meanest face and gritted back, "Drop dead … *Bitch*!"

Everyone froze and waited for the first slap. Before either of us could deliver it, some relative shouted out an even louder

Southern Italian directive and Jennifer beelined for the source. I grabbed my shearling vest and departed.

I remember, as I double-timed home, I was questioning everything I'd done or not done in Jennifer's bedroom. I examined every expression on every face, parsed through every thought that might be going through every mind, and concluded I'd failed miserably. It was a sickening, sinking, hopeless feeling.

Then some kind of numbing agent kicked in. I instinctively slowed to a respectable pace and proceeded to grow another, tougher layer of skin right over the last layer and all the open wounds. It wasn't that I felt relieved. Or even anything like *good*. I just felt located. Forcibly contained. This was the eight-year-old in the Christmas Polaroid.

After Christmas break, it was clear I'd lost some of my social currency. Present posse members began taking unacceptable liberties. Jennifer never said another word but just kept shooting me these penetrating stares that left me functioning like a human computer, constantly recalculating whatever it was I had to say or do to whomever just to maintain whatever status I might still have.

One afternoon, just before that Valentine's Day, she was walking home less than a block ahead of me. I started to slow down, then I came to a dead stop. And then I just kept staring at her, unleashing every scintilla of my hatred for her, trying to crush that bulbous skull into slimy shards with the irresistible force of my infinitely superior mind.

Then the driver had a stroke. That's what they told us. His car jumped the curb and killed her [instantly]. It all happened in slow motion. The shock of her death short-circuited our entire social hierarchy.

At the funeral mass, girls, boys, parents, priests, nuns and total strangers were bawling. I didn't shed a tear. Even at the gravesite where the [sickening] finality of her death was driven home by this exposed hole in the ground, I was dry-eyed.

That night I had my Silver Lady nightmare. It started off like all my other Silver Lady dreams, except in this one, my Silver Lady never glows. She just keeps drifting further away. I keep trying to fly higher, but I already know I can't really fly on my own.

Then I'm falling and the dark river keeps getting closer until I land on it, hard, because it's really some kind of solid plate. It's pitch-black, I can't get my bearings, and I'm too weak to stand up. And then I began to panic [for real].

I woke up in this soaking sweat and started to cry like I can't ever remember crying after that. I did it with my face stuffed in the pillow so Mom wouldn't hear. That was my last Silver Lady nightmare or dream. By the end of third grade I was positive I had everyone and everything under control.

Before reading this letter I'd completely forgotten about that Christmas Day. As I read that first sentence about Desmond's knife, I suddenly had this intense image of Jennifer's bedroom and the look on her face. The memories just spread outward from there. Like milk from a tipped-over glass.

Then, all of a sudden, I felt like I was going to cry again. Like when I was eight. Somehow I stopped myself. But I'm pretty sure [no, I'm positive] I would've cried differently.

[very differently]

— Mirona Guzman

[*Oh my God, Jennifer, I'm <u>so</u> incredibly sorry.*]

13

RAUL'S 3,644TH LETTER

(RL3644-05061974)

*D*ear Mirona,

Well, it finally happened, just like we thought it would. Willy Brandt has resigned as German Chancellor. After Gunther Guillaume's connection with the East German Stasi was discovered, I suppose it was only a matter of time. But are you as surprised as I am at how little support Mr. Brandt has received in the American press? It is as though there is a feeling of relief some other world leader could do something as unacceptable as what President Nixon has been accused of.

What our press seems to be ignoring is that Mr. Brandt was never accused of consciously hiring an East German spy as a close confidant. Given his life history, I can't imagine how he could. But we also know the American press and many American politicians have been uncomfortable with Mr. Brandt's efforts to find areas of cooperation with East Germany and the Soviet bloc nations. They view the idea of reconciliation as foolish or naïve or too dangerous to even consider. Fortunately, the Nobel Peace Prize Committee disagreed with them.

Once an enemy, always an enemy—at least until I defeat you and occupy your country. That was the old Roman model. The senate or the emperors would then encourage intermarriage and a whole range of unifying measures between Romans and conquered locals. It was hegemony preserved by skillful dilution.

Clearly, his detractors' claims notwithstanding, that is not the path Mr. Brandt was suggesting. Moreover, under the Nazis he had seen what happens when a policy of uneasy tolerance is discarded in favor of one of outright elimination. Such fear-driven policies can never produce positive results.

I believe he truly understood the lessons of history and was striving for some kind of common ground, some shared level of dignity among the rulers and the people of those nations. He did not believe common ground was simply what the stronger imposes on the weaker. He believed that mutual respect could generate its own common ground. Not automatically and not easily, of course. As a politician he certainly knew that.

Historically, America has adopted what I like to call the Spanish model. The conquistadors were as devoted to plundering as to proselytizing. Their religious fervor, driven by the presumed intent if not the precise dictates of their superior God, seemed to justify any act that served their earthly ambitions. And we both know how terribly they treated the Puerto Rican natives.

I believe America has replaced a superior God with a superior military-industrial system and relies on that system to justify its actions. American armies work hand in hand with large American corporations throughout the Caribbean and South America. Overwhelmed natives are given a brief chance to embrace an imposed Jeffersonian democracy—which, of course, they cannot. I certainly would not. That is when governments are replaced, laws are changed, and corporate interests become sacred.

Why should America, one of the strongest nations on earth, feel the need to act this way? The only reason I can envision is fear. Imagine that. If I am correct, and I believe I am, then the same fear I witness here, day after day, among people who have no power at all is driving the actions of one of the most powerful nations in history.

We both know this sort of thing cannot continue for any great length of time. Sooner or later history catches up and things change, often in the least desirable ways. There must be a way to change things for the better without destroying everything that came before. There must be something beyond fear and intimidation that all the people of the world can embrace and that can lead to universal peace. I feel like I am getting closer to an answer. As much as I dislike rules—and you know how much I dislike them—I think the answer has to involve rules of some kind. Let's keep thinking about it.

Did you know Willy Brandt was not his real name? He was baptized Herbert Ernst Karl Frohm. His mother was a single parent who worked long hours as a department store cashier and he was raised mostly by her stepfather, Ludwig Frohm. He never met his real father.

In 1933, when the Nazis began persecuting the Social Democrats, he fled Germany for Norway. When he arrived, he changed his name to Willy Brandt to avoid detection by local Nazi secret agents. He came back to Germany briefly in 1936, this time posing as a Norwegian student.

He eventually went off to work as a journalist in Spain and, while there, the German government revoked his citizenship. He then returned to Norway, applied for Norwegian citizenship, and posed as a Norwegian soldier to avoid being identified as a native German by the invading Germans, who arrested him along with other Norwegian soldiers in 1940. That saved his life.

Somehow he escaped to Sweden and after the war returned to Germany to do all the great things he has done.

What a wonderful story.

I will write again tomorrow.

I love you, sweetheart.

Kisses,

Daddy

14

Editor's Commentary On Raul's 3,644th Letter

(RL3644C-05061974-MG1)

May 6, 1974, was the day I got back from our junior class trip to New York City after figuring out who I really was. At the time I was still an inmate at Saint Bridget's Catholic Grammar School and High School, just two blocks from our place in Chicago. Mom wasn't even a little bit religious, but felt safer with me tucked away in a culturally familiar institution.

Getting on the bus to New York was going to require a signed parental consent form, and I knew right off the bat that would be a massive problem. By now my mother could barely speak the words "New York City." It was the place—she felt periodically obliged to reconfirm—where my alleged father had died in a traffic accident, but over the years it had become increasingly clear there was a much deeper backstory.

I'd long mastered the art of wielding the daddy question like a surgical weapon. A few quick slashes left her bent and bleeding but, somehow, she'd never break—which made it even clearer that the truth of my genesis could only be confirmed in the Big Apple. In a pre-digital, pre-internet world, that left me exactly one option.

Forging her perfectly legible signature was simple enough. And, of course, my teachers never suspected a thing, especially not from their top student. All that was left was to pack a bag and sneak out of the house at 5 a.m. on May 3. Mom never made it home from work at night before 7:45, so I had plenty of time to rehearse my escape.

During the trip I regaled our most gullible chaperone with my lifelong dreams about hunting down the missing information on my deceased father that would ["Finally!"] help Mom get full closure after ["*lo*,"] so many years. To do it, I'd have to visit the Municipal Building, which wasn't on our itinerary. Ms. Lubcik was tearing up as she hugged me.

That first night I snuck out of my hotel room around midnight and eventually wandered into this very dark bar somewhere on Seventh Avenue. I was no stranger to drinking illegally, but found my skin tone always drew more initial attention than the exotic looks and great body I was always told I had. The solution was to quickly order my first Brandy Alexander in perfected American with ultimate graciousness. Bartenders and their customers were instantly disoriented and I almost never got proofed.

The guy who picked me up was probably in his early thirties. He was White [I only socialized with White boys], Jewish, *"dressed in a suit/sorta cute,"* and said he worked in the fashion industry.

We took a freight elevator up to this factory space in the same building and had sex on a pattern-cutting table. I was still a technical virgin and a little nervous, but nowhere near as nervous as he was. This was obviously his first tryst with a non-Caucasian and, the rag business being what it was, most probably his first with a nonwhore. He didn't know what to expect.

Five minutes later, as I casually tucked my panties into my purse, I instructed him [in blasé post-coital British] to call me a limousine. The idiot lifted the receiver so fast he knocked the phone off his desk.

We waited in front of the building in dead silence. Just as the limo pulled up, he turned and asked my name. I looked at him with a look I'd eventually perfect: "You don't need to know." Those words from the mouth of the youngest girl in junior year.

Later that morning I headed downtown to the Municipal Building on my own. In those days it held microfiche records of all the births and deaths in the five boroughs of New York City.

It took surprisingly little time to locate Miron Andrej Podluski. The records said he'd died of a gunshot wound on West 64th

Street at 6:45 p.m. on July 23, 1958. That's all there was, but it was more than enough to confirm my mother was a filthy liar.

I rejoined the group at the 42nd Street Library and headed for the newspaper archives area. It housed microfilm copies of local and national newspapers dating back to the nineteenth century, and my hope was there'd been local coverage of the murder I'd just uncovered.

And there was, lots of it. But the coverage was less about the murder than the trial that followed a few months later. An issue of the *New York Daily Mirror* from December of 1958 featured a banner headline that read "The West Side Latin Lover." Below the headline was a picture of my mother racing down the steps of the State Supreme Court building at Foley Square with Aunt Lydia trying to cover her face. A swarm of reporters was hot on their trail.

The story was as lurid and one-sided as they get. My mother was the impregnated Latina temptress who had jilted her junkie boyfriend who, in turn, had murdered her secret lover. There was an artist's rendering of Mom on the witness stand, her modestly draped belly bulging with me as she pointed an accusing finger at my father.

There were two photographs. One was a studio headshot of Miron Andrej Podluski. He was a handsome, fair-skinned man. The other was this mis-lit mug shot of dazed and darkened Raul Guzman with the entire left side of his face covered by a perfectly exposed white gauze bandage. I recognized him instantly from the photo at Aunt Lydia's.

According to the newspaper account, Raul had attempted suicide by shooting himself in the mouth after killing Miron and trying to kill my mother. His drug-crazed aim was off and he'd instead removed a substantial chunk of left cheek. The *Daily Mirror* portrayed it as a case of too-little-too-late remorse on the part of a natural-born killer.

What actually happened is a bit more nuanced. Benito, my father's alpha drug buddy, had somehow identified Miron as a gay man and was goading my father to murder him. It should be noted: There could be few scenarios more existentially threatening to a macho Latino than the thought of an identifiably gay man dating his ex-girlfriend. Granted, Mom wasn't Benito's ex-girlfriend, but he'd developed these love-hate feelings about her he'd never be able to express and that were undoubtedly intensified by his own drug-addled chemistry. Benito's malleable acolyte would set things straight.

Around this same time my mother had [in her words] seduced Raul. It was the first time they'd had sex since San Juan. She knew he was still using drugs but remained hopelessly in love with him and couldn't resist making one final attempt to reactivate his pre-druggie persona.

It worked—for a few hours, anyway. My father snuck away late that night [after stealing one hundred and twenty-eight dollars from an envelope hidden in the furthest recesses of one of her dresser drawers] and dropped out of sight. A few weeks later, Mom realized she was pregnant. Illegally aborting his child was out of the question, so when Miron suggested a marriage of convenience, she jumped at the opportunity.

Raul had a gun [supplied by Benito] in his elevated hand as he stood across the street from my mother and Miron. Stoned as he was, he says he was prepared to use it. He didn't know they'd already made plans to marry. The way he describes it, when he saw the flash of the diamond engagement ring on my mother's finger, the vengeance somehow drained out of him; some "surviving patch of clarity" allowed him to recognize the immorality of his intentions and he slowly lowered the gun to his side [coincidentally eliminating any basis for a felony murder charge].

Benito and two other druggies were watching all this unfold from the safe confines of a double-parked stolen sedan. As Raul lowered his hand, the sedan suddenly screeched forward, then came to a screeching halt between Raul on one side and my mother and Miron on the other. Benito rolled down the rear window nearest my father, called him a *maricón* (faggot), and grabbed the gun. The next thing Raul remembered was the sound of two gunshots. My mother was sitting in Miron's car and remembers seeing the flashes coming out of the sedan's other rear window the instant before both front windows of Miron's car shattered, although she couldn't say who actually fired the shots.

Raul had no recollection of how the gun got back into his hand. The only rational explanation is Benito put it there after he fired the fatal bullet. Then the sedan sped off.

In his drugged-out state, when my father finally recognized neither my mother nor Miron were where they'd been a moment earlier [Miron was dead on the sidewalk behind his car; Mom was hunkered down on the front seat], he concluded he'd committed a double murder. He inserted the gun barrel into his gaping mouth and was about to perforate his medulla and cerebellum when Aunt Lydia screamed his name from her third-floor window. His head jerked, the gun fired, but the bullet passed through his cheek instead of his brain.

Of course, I knew none of these details as I sat shaking and blubbering in front of a microfilm reader in the New York Public Library. I knew only what readers of the *New York Daily Mirror* were prepared and expected to believe.

Still, I had the presence of mind to get a copy of the article. As much as it was evidence of my shameful genesis, it was also conclusive proof of Mom's mendacity. Now I desperately longed for the refuge of my anger and for that next layer of skin to grow.

On the trip back to Chicago, I sat by myself at a window seat near the rear of the bus. My current posse must have sensed something was amiss but knew enough not to encroach.

I remember opening the notebook where I'd stuck the photocopy and just staring at the picture of Raul's bandaged face. Suddenly [finally] the anger recongealed. It began with ballpoint scribbles on his bandage; then on his forehead; then glancing blows to the neck and ears; then full-force stabs at the eyes. I stabbed him so hard the ballpoint broke in my hand and a thick glob of black ink smeared the side of my fist. I began pounding his face like an enraged rubber stamp.

Two former posse members were sitting across the aisle one row back, just staring. As I finally became aware of them, I felt the saliva dripping from my mouth and the tears running down my cheeks. I don't know how but, somehow, I forced myself under control and casually began looking out the window.

[And no one—not a single one of my teachers, posse members past or present, or any of my other classmates—ever dared bring up a word about any of this.[3]]

It was nearly midnight when I got home. The door at the top of the stairs was open and Mom was just standing there, fully dressed, awaiting the prodigal daughter. I found out later she'd called my school in a [contained] panic to report I hadn't come home that first evening. The school secretary had stayed late to answer calls from concerned, permission-granting parents wanting to know the status of our bus. When she took Mom's call, she apparently translated her polite inquiry into the same kind of question she'd been fielding all evening. My mother got the standard update on the bus and its authorized occupants and realized

----

3 To my face.

what I'd done. Rather than out me on the spot, she calmly drew a bucketful from her bottomless reservoir of self-control, politely thanked the school secretary, and patiently awaited my return. We were far more alike than either of us realized.

It began with the disciplinary digit—which normally appeared after all attempts at reason had been exhausted and was typically accompanied by an archipelago of disjointed words. This time it was something like, "You! … You … little you… you will … *never* …," all at a volume respecting Uncle Peter's established sleep habits.

I'd prepared a statement of my own. Before she could break out of syncopation I screamed, "*Shut* … the *fuck* … *up*!!"

The standing rules of engagement collapsed. I'm pretty sure the look on her face was embarrassment more than shock. It took her a few seconds to improvise a new plan of action and hit the reset button, at which point the disciplinary digit fanned out into a first-ever opened palm. She took a sputtering step toward me.

I took a step of my own, stuck my face directly into hers, and in a gurgling mockery of my five-year-old voice: "Mommy, where's my daddy?" And then, from somewhere well beyond the top of my lungs: "*Huh*!!!???"

Not long ago, Mom told me that second scream was identical to the one issued by my 19-year-old stoned father as he threw a copy of *Modern Detective Stories* magazine in her face [about ten minutes before she seduced him]. My mother happened to be on the cover dressed in a scanty negligee and fending off the assault of some faceless assassin. The sound froze her now as it froze her then.

At that moment, I think I actually wanted her to slap me. It might've reversed whatever had just happened and reestablished some semblance of normalcy. With nothing left to do, I marched into my bedroom and slammed the door shut with all my might.

Then I stood there, frozen, for what must have been ten minutes just waiting to hear any kind of sound. There was none. Mom was holding her hands over her mouth as the tears streamed down her face. As though the sound of her crying might tip off the ADA.

I was already a skilled practitioner of the Spanish model. Fear-Act Out was my superior system. I used it to justify an indecent number of unsavory acts and, a bit later in life, a few arguably criminal ones. Raul might have been trying to remind me it didn't have to be that way. Greatness, he hinted, could still come from the likes of me.

Still, the first time I read this letter, I was a little bored. Yes, I knew who Willy Brandt was and, no, I wasn't a big fan. I had the same ambivalent opinion of him as most other Americans who were fed the same ambivalent coverage about his chancellorship. And I certainly got the hard-to-miss analogies between his background and my own.

Then I read that sentence near the end: "*That saved his life.*" It stopped me dead in my tracks. I found myself rereading it several times. The next thing I did was check the date of the letter.

And then the memories flooded back, just as they had on several prior occasions and would on many others. Apparently that sentence was the trip wire that reenergized one of those implanted kernels of comprehension Gina talks about.

She also describes them as soft beacons glowing just strongly enough to guide me to the next beacon, and then the next.

Like being led without knowing it.

[Because if I'd known …]

— Mirona Guzman

15

RAUL'S 3,827TH LETTER

(RL3827-11051974)

Dear Mirona,

You know I'm not big on rules. And you know how I have fought the idea of stating any truism as a rule, and especially as a prohibition. But if there had to be just one, I think this is it.

It came to me in a spontaneous meditation while I was correcting papers this morning. The entire structure was there, and it was perfect! I had to stop everything and begin searching for the words. It must have taken me three hours, and once I had them, they almost sounded too simple. But we know better, don't we?

Here they are, sweetheart:

"You may not pass along the hurtful things that were passed on to you."

The words are so easy! And yet they bring all the elements together. Most importantly, they meet the universality test. I know it at the core of my being!

Start with us. Think about all the things you know about me and all the things I have done. Now, ask yourself, what are the things I passed along to you? Which of them was hurtful? When did you know? How did you know?

Can you understand why those things were passed to you? Can you imagine the hurt and the pain inside the person who gave them to you? And can you imagine how you might pass them on and what would happen to the next recipient if you did?

Now reread the rule. You see? It's all there! Even the most cursory reading forces a consideration of every one of the funda- mental structural and transmission elements. That means anyone can work with it—provided, of course, they don't dismiss it out of hand as something so simple and self-evident that it deserves no further examination.

That also means the initial presentation of the Rule must be thoughtful and supportive. It cannot simply be injected into a conversation. I know, I am getting way ahead of myself, but these are things that deeply concern me. Knowing me as you do, you can understand why!

Lately I have been in a meditative state for as many as two hours a day. A young Tendai Buddhist monk, Seth Feinman, began joining me in meditation about a month ago. Seth is only in his mid-twenties and very bright. He studied Buddhism and was recently ordained in Japan, where Tendai is the major Buddhist sect. Seth now spends a substantial part of his time visiting and counseling inmates at several regional prisons.

Seth believes meditation should be more structured, at least as to when and how it begins. Beyond that, he believes the goal of meditation is to become one with the nothingness so beautifully described in the Buddhist Heart Sutra. My "natural" meditations, as he calls them, are always focused on "something," some specific image not unlike the image that produced the Rule. Seth says he is fascinated by my meditations and is presently seeking a way to emulate them. I am honored by his interest.

As you can tell from his name, Seth is not Japanese. In fact, he is the son of Orthodox Jewish parents from Brooklyn and says he is still a practicing Jew. Imagine that. His adoption of Buddhism works perfectly well with his established religious tradition. He and I have also been exploring why Buddhism—or, at least, Tendai Buddhism—makes this possible. The answer seems to lie in Tendai's ability to function equally well as a philosophy and a religion. It has no sectarian codes that violate the boundaries of Judaism or any other religion. Instead, it operates primarily on a spiritual level that, according to Tendai, is common to all sentient beings and fosters a moral code that transcends any theology or sectarian creed.

Mirona, this is exactly how I envision the Rule operating! Its application is not limited to any group of people or subject to any religious test. All it asks is that we not hurt anyone and embrace all the implications of that mandate. What request could be more universally understood and accepted?

The problem lies in how people will interpret "not passing along hurtful things." Many people will imagine it simply means not exposing their children to negative behaviors. So a drug addict will never shoot up in front of his kids. Or a killer will make certain his kids never suspect the violence he is capable of.

Yet, amazingly, the worst behaviors of parents are often adopted by their children, no matter how carefully they think they have hidden them. I have heard the same story told here on countless occasions. I have watched the toughest men weep helplessly when they realized their children were following in their footsteps.

That is what is so amazing about the Rule. When it came to me, it included a vision of how the transmission of hurtful things could be limited. It has nothing to do with hiding negative behavior, although it will help stop that behavior in the long run.

You see, Mirona, these negative behaviors are just the final manifestation of something far deeper. The source of these behaviors exists on an energetic level. For lack of a better term, I will call them negative frequencies. They are the energetic embodiment of the fear you and I have discussed so many times. We both know our Souls are designed to operate optimally in an environment of pure love, but if love is suppressed, it is automatically replaced by some variant of unchecked fear. And that amplified fear is what energizes negative behavior. Most people would have a difficult time making a direct connection between their deepest, nameless fears and their negative behaviors. But, as we have both seen, that is just how it works.

If fear is transmitted generationally through energetic means, as I now truly believe it is, then all we have to do is find a way to eliminate or neutralize that fear in the carrier and the transmission process will be stopped in its tracks. The question is, how do we do that? I know it involves some form of energetic "cleansing," but I do not know exactly how it would work. My instincts tell me it will involve meditation or perhaps some other form of spiritual intervention. When Seth comes tomorrow, I plan to discuss it with him. He will sense which way to proceed.

Mirona, think of what would happen if even twenty percent of the world followed the Rule. The jails would begin to empty out. Poverty, hunger, and ignorance would begin to disappear. And war would be impossible. Imagine that! All because we stopped passing on the hurtful things that were passed on to us.

And there is yet another wonderful thing about the Rule. Because it operates on an energetic level, it is not subject to time constraints! Negative frequencies will be amenable to intervention, no matter how young or old a person is or how long the hurt has existed. The healing process can be initiated at any time by or with anyone, no matter how hopeless or how dire their circumstances.

I have to be careful not to let all of this overwhelm me. I have to take it one step at a time and work out all the details. But, Mirona, do you understand what this means? It means there is always hope! For everyone! Always!

And it means it is never too late to stop passing on the pain. In fact, that is how you begin to heal yourself. Yes! Now I know it, just as I am writing this.

It is all connected. And I know it sounds hard to believe. But you will! Trust me, sweetheart, you will. It is never too late!

I'll write again tomorrow.

I love you, sweetheart.

Kisses,

Daddy

16

EDITOR'S COMMENTARY ON RAUL'S 3,827TH LETTER

(RL3827C-11051974-MG1)

If you had to rank my father's letters in order of importance, RL3827 would be at the top of the list, and for good reason. Few things in Raul's writings could be more significant than his first statement of the First Rule.

But what struck me most the first time I read it was its tone. It's the only time in all his writings he uses exclamation points. Obviously he was excited by his discoveries but, especially toward the end, there's also this growing urgency in his voice. He may have sensed the darkness descending on my life and he came as close as he ever did to warning me about it outright. Gina says he was showing me the brightest possible image of his distant beacons as I entered into a period of profound spiritual blindness.

It was my senior year at St. Bridget's and six months after the New York City trip. By now my relationship with Mom had pretty much normalized if only because she was too classy to sustain a grudge.

We'd taken the National Merit Scholarship exam at the end of junior year, and in those days the results were announced sometime before the following Thanksgiving. I already knew I was one of the four finalists at our school. A full scholarship would mean full tuition plus room and board at any U.S. college or university where the recipient had been accepted. When Ms. Kaczmarczyk announced there'd be an assembly of all junior and senior girls in one hour, we knew she'd gotten the results.

Althea was one of the finalists. By some miracle she'd managed to maintain both her academic focus and her sanity. I no longer tortured her openly, but I could still change her vector with a dirty look and occasionally did it to amuse current posse members.

At the assembly the four of us stood at attention while Ms. Kaczmarczyk ran off a litany of our academic achievements. I remember the insecurity on the faces of the other three and took the opportunity to serve up some of my most demoralizing stares.

I won the only full scholarship. The audience must have applauded me for close to thirty seconds. My demoralizing continued on autopilot and two of the other finalists were irreversibly pulverized.

But not Althea. She was looking right at me the whole time, smiling and applauding with an openness and a sincerity that was completely unanticipated. My stare meant nothing to her. It reflected back into my brain and exploded.

Suddenly I felt a hopelessness—an emptiness—worse than the one I felt walking home from Jennifer's. The sensation was worse than the worst moment of my Silver Lady nightmare. There was no one to defeat, nothing to push back against, no new layer of skin quick or thick enough to cover it all. I panicked. [And, of course, I managed a convincing smile.]

The seniors were dismissed for the day right after that. I raced home, changed into my hot purple minidress and my Frye boots, and headed for Old Town. The emptiness hadn't eased one bit, but by now I'd objectified it in my mind and I was positive I knew how to defeat it.

There was this hole-in-the-wall bar that attracted questionable types. I was a semi-regular. My normal hours were from about 5:40 to 6:30, which got me home no later than 7:10, in plenty of time to change my clothes, my breath, and the smallest piece of my persona. The evening bartender never proofed.

Now it was only around 2:00. The place was nearly empty and the day bartender was a complete stranger. Emilio was sitting a few stools away with his slick black hair, almost black eyes, and that shortish, muscular box of a body. He must've been in his early twenties. I'd seen him a few times before, mostly as I was coming and he was going. It was pretty obvious I turned him on and equally obvious some clause in the Mafioso rule book stipulated he had to keep it in his pants, at least with girls like me.

I mustered up my most sophisticated voice and ordered my leadoff Brandy Alexander. The bartender hesitated and asked for proof. Before I could run the calculations, Emilio mumbled something like "*Ay*" as he made eye contact with the guy, then gave the slightest head-tick in my direction. Drink one materialized, followed a hard chug later by a level-one buzz.

Emilio had no real personality and about as much intellectual prowess as any low-level Mafia soldier would ever need. He told me he delivered "*packages*" for his uncle and seemed to appreciate that I got it without asking pesky questions. He'd be dead before thirty, but he was oozing power right now. And right now I desperately needed to push off of it.

By around 5:30 I was thoroughly sloshed and making out with him in the front seat of his Eldorado. He was rough and ripping through my panty hose, which was fine by me. Suddenly I had this demented thought. I pushed him away and slur-gushed, "Less go-duh *my* place!" He shot back this unexpectedly calculating stare, then glanced at his watch: "I gotta make a phone call innuh half hour, y'unnerstan'?"

Emilio screwed like he was in this big, empty stadium all by himself. About two minutes in [I remember this so clearly] he hesitated, then quickened his pace, then sort of pulled out as he came, then rested his weight on me for a few more panting seconds, then rolled off and checked his watch again. A moment later the overwhelming emptiness was back.

A moment after that, I heard the downstairs door open. I'd seen Uncle Peter's car in the driveway, so it had to be my mother. This was infinitely earlier than she ever came home.

I think I whispered, "Oh shit!" Emilio produced a gun out of nowhere and an uninflected, "Who's dat." I remember whispering him to shut the fuck up as I closed my bedroom door as quietly as I could. By then Mom was up the stairs opening the front door. I'm pretty sure she called my name as she walked in.

Emilio was surprisingly quick for a box and was already zippering his fly when she opened my bedroom door. I was in my panties, still trying to match up the first button and hole on one of my tops. Everyone froze.

She barely even glanced at him. He read the situation perfectly, somehow managed to slink around her, and raced down the stairs [presumably to make his phone call from a safer location].

The staring contest continued. The emptiness was dropping through me like a sinkhole and I desperately needed something to stop the sensation. It would either be a total attack or a total collapse.

I've mentioned how just a sentence or a phrase from one of my father's letters can bring the memories back for me. The sentence that did it in this letter came early on. Just after Raul finishes talking about the spontaneous meditation that produced the image of the Rule, he adds, "*I had to stop everything and begin searching for the words.*" As I read that, the memory of my emptiness and everything else about that November evening came flooding in, but I have almost no memory of the actual words exchanged between my mother and me, except for one. Gina calls it a self-protective energetic blockage.

What follows is based on my mother's painfully accurate recollections. Apparently I began with, "What? Why don't you just come out and say it? No, wait! Say it in Spanish! Ya think I won't unnerstan'? Yer one hundred percent SPIC *slut*!?"

That got her juices flowing, but she still started off in first gear with, "You don't talk to me like that!" And that wasn't nearly enough to push off against. I guess I was too drunk to go through our normal fermentation process, and I started walking toward her. She started backing up.

"Whussa matter? Ya forgot how to *say* it? S'gotta be a nasty word somewhere in that … *perf*ect … white … *pack*age!" That last line must've really frightened her. She backed all the way into the hallway, waving a fist and hissing a muffled, "Shut up! Shut up!" I was nowhere near satisfied. I grabbed her fist and held it up to my face. "Hey, maybe if you slam some ugly … darkie … *puss* … it'll just *pop* outta ya!" And then, she says, I started mocking her in a bad Puerto Rican accent: "*Co'mahn, Teresa, co'mahn!*" It still wasn't enough. I started whacking myself in the face with her fist and vaguely remember the sensation of fighting for control of her hand.

She won it back. There was this insane pause while we both just stood there, panting. No, still not nearly enough.

Finally, it just screamed out of me: *"Nail the fucking little Black whore!!!"*

That lit up all the right neurons. I have this perfect recollection of her eyes bulging like hard-boiled eggs as she screamed *"Putita!!!"* at the top of her lungs and smacked my face with every ounce of her strength. The word means "little whore" in Spanish. It's the same word her mother used when she learned Mom was pregnant with me. Neither of us knew I'd have my first abortion in about seven weeks.

My mother says we just stood there, frozen. Then I chuckled and said, "So *dat's* the word!"—at which point I turned and headed for my room.

Ah, but I'd omitted the *coup de grace*. She says I turned back and in this horribly controlled voice: "Oh, by the way, I won a full National Merit Scholarship. I'm outta yer life fer*ev*er … Missus *Guzz*-min."

I staggered back into my bedroom and slammed the door shut, probably more out of drunken clumsiness than anything else. Mom says she stood there on the other side and cried like she hadn't cried in years. At some point I must've collapsed on the bed and passed out. That's where I found myself in my panties and misbuttoned blouse when I woke up in the middle of the night to puke.

Things changed after that. I came and went pretty much as I liked and made no serious effort to hide my drinking or my sexuality. My mother was reduced to some hapless observer who'd set a series of events in motion and could only stare as they played out. In one of the few exchanges before I left, I reminded her I'd be attending Columbia University, "in New York City." Without looking up, she barely whispered, "Of course."

Then I was gone. There was no contact, but it would be a complete fabrication to say she was out of my life. I devoted a great deal of energy to marginalizing my memories of her and my father, all to no avail. Either of them could be plucked out of my subconscious at any moment by even the most mundane thoughts or events.

Gina talks about the need for forgiveness and how it's only through the unconditional forgiveness of the wrongs of both our ancestors and ourselves that we achieve true dignity in our lives. I've apologized to my mother many times for the awful things I said and did that night. Mom has forgiven me. Many times.

Mom has also asked my forgiveness for hitting me and calling me a whore. I've forgiven her, or at least I've wanted to forgive her, but I've never really achieved a sense of dignity about it. Somehow, maybe, if I could just remember it all on my own and work through it, I might be able to let it go completely.

Gina says I keep redraining only a part of the frequency that supports my guilt and self-loathing and always retain enough to regenerate the embodiment of my pain whenever memories of emptiness rise to the surface. Patience and love. That's her infuriating prescription. Of course, she's right.

And I know I should, but I won't even try to discuss the First Rule except to say it makes perfect sense when you think about it.

[And "thinking about it" is about as far as this little whore's ever going to get anyway.]

— Mirona Guzman

[But thank you for those distant beacons just the same.]

17

DR. GINA GILFORD'S COMMENTARY ON RAUL'S 3,827TH LETTER

(RL3827C-11051974-GG2)

RL3827 is one of the most important documents ever written. So much more than a functional description of Universal Energy, it is the inductive vision of a brilliantly inspired Soul and the seminal statement of need for a practical methodology to deliver the benefits of Universal Energy through Energy Medicine to our entire planet.

The idea of such a methodology would have struck our distant ancestors as very strange. After all, they would have reasoned, we are Energy beings who derive our very existence from the energetic forces that define and bind us. What need is there for a distribution methodology? Energy is naturally self-distributive.

Nonetheless, today, that need exists. And while the nature of Energy remains unchanged, the accurate perception and comprehension of its role has diminished substantially in Western cultures and in American culture particularly. This reduced comprehension has been long-term, the product of many factors and the cause of many problems.

Prior to the expansion of agrarian cultures, our Universal Energy was at the root of all religious, scientific, medical, and governance processes. We illustrate its cyclic ancient/modern role in the CG title sequence created for *Energy With Doctor Gina*.

The emergence of cities and the development of more complex, interdependent societies brought about the need for more behavioral conformity. Religious narratives emerged. While energetically influenced, they included a range of parochial social and moral mandates and typically located an anthropomorphic God or Gods at the top of a supernatural governance pyramid. An earthly, co-ruling priesthood was incorporated into that pyramid and was granted exclusive knowledge of sacred mysteries and the exclusive right to perform key sacred rituals.

While their energetic roots and rationales may have been shared, early religions emphasized their differences. Those differences were most probably an effective proselytizing tool and promoted necessary cohesion within cities and states in regular conflict with other cities and states. The Jews, for example, worshipped a single God who, to their good fortune and the presumed dismay of their bellicose neighbors, had established a personal and exclusive relationship with the Jewish people. Nonetheless, their monotheism was most probably an extension of Hindu monotheism minus its numerous metaphorical avatars.

Christianity adopted major variations on both the personal and functional aspects of the Hindu Trinity (Brahma, Vishnu, Shiva). Then, going a major step beyond Judaism, it asserted (with a nod to Egypt and Rome) that a member of its divine Trinity had been incarnated as a historical human personage. Ever conscious of that member's Jewish roots, Christianity declared itself the beneficiary of a "new covenant" superseding the covenant God had made with the Jews and one focusing on the after-death salvation of the soul, an area of ambiguity in Jewish writings. This declaration all but established institutionalized anti-Semitism while engendering a series of internal theological and sometimes military battles that would not be resolved until the early fourth century by the Roman Emperor Constantine. (Unremarkably, the Roman Catholic organizational structure evolved into, and remains, an almost perfect replica of the Roman imperial model. Constantine remained a major power within the now official Christian church even as he continued to offer sacrifices to the old Roman Gods.)

Organized religions, as one of my theology professors so often reminded us, are divine-human institutions. And while the divine may be given spoken precedence, religious institutions can only be sustained through the elevation of their human component. The God embedded in these human structures, followers' claims of His universality notwithstanding, invariably takes on highly sectarian characteristics and is all too often called on to sanction activities in direct conflict with sacred narratives.

All major religions are also what I term *unilistic* at their roots. Minus the sectarian narratives and social dicta, all begin with the postulation of an omnipotent God beyond the scope of human comprehension characterized by an unbridled capacity for love and an intimate involvement with every aspect and element of creation.

The same definition could be applied to Universal Energy, the stuff that has been present from before the first instant of creation and that defines, binds, and empowers everyone and everything. In fact, the terms God and Energy would be perfectly interchangeable were it not for the anthropomorphic, sectarian limitations placed on God.

The term Energy, likewise, has long been miscategorized as referring to the purely scientific and being at loggerheads with all things religious. Yet we are edging ever closer to the realization that there is no practical distinction between the empirical findings of modern science and the tenets of spirituality. To assert one's spirituality is to say nothing more than, "I am connected to all of creation." The connective mechanism, it winds up, is the same Energy shared by God and science.

Over time the nonsectarian, energetic component of God has been organizationally downplayed to the point where it is little more than a basis for internal reflection (and possible conflict) for only the truest of believers. The rank and file seem content to accept theological narratives and dicta as [too often mis-] interpreted by organizational hierarchies and, by and large, do not bother themselves with obvious contradictions that lie just beneath the surface.

Still, all sentient beings are naturally drawn to their energetic roots and the commonalities inherent in those roots. Social, political, and religious prohibitions notwithstanding, our American ancestors were begrudgingly fascinated by the organization-free animism and spirit beliefs of the races under their control. Unwilling or unable to recognize that same Energy in the nature of a politicized God, they were increasingly drawn to smaller manifestations of energetic power that, while in technical conflict with Christian tenets, remained deeply compelling. For that reason and others, to this day, most Americans cautiously express a belief in some combination of energetic prognostication, talismans, imposed curses, poltergeists, energetic healings and the like. Unfortunately, such piecemeal perceptions and beliefs tend to confine Energy to the realm of the spooky.

An accurate comprehension of our common energetic heritage and a broad dissemination of its healing powers through Energy Medicine have always been my primary goals. In the seven years since *Energy With Doctor Gina* was first broadcast, I have witnessed a steadily increasing comprehension of Universal Energy among Americans and others, understandably accompanied by some voices of disagreement and dissent. By and large, those voices have been civil and many have been given a fair hearing on my show.

Recently, however, those voices have multiplied and evolved into a dissonant chorus calling for, among other things, the cancellation of my show, the criminalization of Energy Medicine, and my immediate incarceration or worse. This has happened in concert with a series of what, until very recently, would have been considered unthinkable acts. We have watched the United States House of Representatives riot after a Capitol police officer was shot to death on the floor of Congress by an elected Republican official.

We then watched the House Democratic majority unilaterally decertify the original electoral vote confirming the election of the president, followed by the forcible occupation of the Oval Office by the vice president and his supporters even as most of the House Republican Caucus continues its boycott of all legislative functions. Just yesterday we witnessed an attack on Democratic National Committee headquarters and the tragic deaths of 46 civilians and uniformed service people.

Most disturbing of all, if such things can even be categorized, is the increasing evidence that elements of the military, the police, and other weapons-carrying authorities throughout the country are in open conflict with one another and within their own ranks, and are forming coalitions with other public and private weapons-carrying entities.

How could all this happen? Some blame it on NASA's announcement of two warring races of sentient life in the internal ocean of Europa. More accurately, it is the product of the barely contained fears and other negative frequencies now fully realized and reflexively acted upon by key segments of our society in response to the changes unleashed by that discovery.

For those of us in the energetic community, beyond the thrill of finding another sentient life-form so close to our own planet, there was the thrill of establishing energetic contact with several members of one of the races. Our Souls were linked over a distance of more than five hundred million miles. What I personally experienced was an innocent openness and a desire to understand interspersed with powerful cries for help. The experience was both exhilarating and heartrending at the same time.

I was also thrilled to learn that we were not alone in our experiences and reactions. Grete Pedersen's first appearance on the *Christiane Amanpour Show* introduced us to the activities of the Foundation for Change, their detection of an energetic shift in our planet's core frequency, and their certainty that it portended a major, positive change in the energetic integrity of the entire planet. Like everyone else, we had seen Grete's beautiful images on the Benetton "Change" advertisements that began to appear just before the first NASA announcement, and we immediately sensed we were being prepared for something more than a new line of sports clothing.

Grete referred to the discovery of sentient life as one of many possible "precipitating events" the Foundation for Change was preparing for. They had no advance knowledge that sentient life would actually be discovered.

Apparently the military, or those elements of the military now under the exclusive jurisdiction of the acting secretary of defense, did not accept this version of the facts. They accused the Foundation for Change of long-distance "energetic collaboration" with the Europans and pointed to the destruction of our probe by one of the two races as proof of a collective hostile intent.

At the other extreme, a growing number of Jewish, Christian, and Muslim clergy have joined the ranks of the deniers, insisting that the first NASA press release announcing the discovery of sentient life was fabricated in collusion with the Foundation for Change in an effort to promote an anti-religious agenda. It is one of the few things they seem to agree on. According to a spokesperson for the American Bishops' Conference, "If God had intended to create another form of intelligent life, He would have first alerted His Church to His intentions through Divine Revelation."

I have expressed my support for the tenets and activities of the Foundation for Change on several recent shows. Then, early this morning, I received a phone call from one of my producers telling me she had been informed by a representative of the acting secretary of defense that we would be taping our last *Energy With Doctor Gina* segment this evening. The reason given was the acting secretary could no longer guarantee my safety and that of my staff.

At the time of the call I was standing in my partially ransacked office. I say partially because it was clear the individual or group responsible for the act was more interested in conveying a message than destroying property.

Years ago I had a simple exhibit constructed for one of my seminars. It consisted of a clear plastic tube about six inches in diameter and bent into the shape of the letter "U." Each of the arms was about two feet long and filled halfway up with water. Floating in each of the arms was a large plastic disk, one marked with the word "love" and the other with "fear." Because water finds its own level, the two disks remained perfectly parallel.

During the seminar, I would use a kind of plunger to depress one disk or the other. As "fear" was suppressed, "love" would rise, and vice versa. The point I made was that our Souls operate in much the same way. To emanate love, we must exercise our wills, suppress our fears, and accept the changes that follow or run the risk that our fears and their variants will overwhelm our capacity to love and to accommodate all the avatars of love.

The only things destroyed in my office were the chair I sit in to conduct private sessions and my love-fear exhibit. On the wall behind the table where the exhibit sat, someone spray-painted an inverted letter "U" and the words "All who blaspheme die in fear!"

I was not aware the acting secretary of defense was responsible for my safety. I am now very much aware my safety is in no way guaranteed by any source. Several of my staff have urged me to forgo this evening's taping and, effectively, go into hiding. I cannot and will not do that. To do so would undermine not only my own credibility but everything I have communicated about our common energetic heritage and the role of Energy Medicine.

More than that, it would diminish if not wholly undermine the significance of Raul Guzman's work. Raul effectively predicted the civil disintegration we are beginning to experience. His meticulously described methodology for identifying and neutralizing the large-scale transmission of negative energetic frequencies anticipated circumstances precisely such as these. Beyond this, I know in the deepest part of my being that Raul's First Rule offers the only viable path to reversing our current state of affairs or, perhaps, to extricating ourselves from the worst of what may come.

My energetic gifts do not include precise prognostication, but I do not need that kind of gift to know I have reason to be concerned. At the same time, I am not fearful. And because I am not fearful, I can extend my love and my fondest wishes to all who are dear to me, to all who have listened to my words in the past and to all who may read these words in the future.

I urge anyone reading this book, whenever and under whatever circumstances you may be reading it, to please consider following Raul's First Rule. It offers our last best hope. It is my privilege to repeat it and its corollary here: "*You may not pass along the hurtful things that were passed on to you. You must pass along the good things that were passed on to you.*"

Let us embrace and give thanks to the Infinite Transcendence, the Loving Oneness, beyond all books, institutions, and theologies for the privilege of serving in a way that many more will be blessed to serve. May we all be instruments for the rekindling of genuine hope. And may we always know the joys of endless compassion, total dedication, and deepest love.

— *Gina Gilford*

18

Editor's Note

I received this commentary in an email at about 3:00 yesterday after-noon, an hour before Gina tapes. It's a nearly complete revision of her original commentary on RL3827 and ends with the beautiful blessing she recites at the conclusion of every show she's ever done.

Gina was doing one final energetic review of my trimmed-down still nameless book, finally scheduled for publication in three weeks. Her cover email was unusually brief: "Dearest Mirona, Please replace my commentary to RL3827 with the attached. Change nothing else in the book and promise me you will write its epilogue. Love and Blessings, Always, Gina."

At about 5:45 I received a phone call from one of her segment producers, Matthew Warner, telling me Gina, her current guest, and several of her staff and crew, including Matthew's girlfriend, Lisa, had been murdered on the set. Two gunmen sitting in opposite parts of the studio audience had somehow concealed automatic weapons and opened fire midway through the taping. Matthew wasn't on the set. Blake was standing just on the far edge with Tim Koralis, the assistant director, and was grazed in the arm. Tim was killed. The gunmen escaped. Matthew called the police, but uniformed soldiers showed up to remove the bodies. They wouldn't say where they were being taken.

Things have gotten totally chaotic since then. Matthew finally called back a little while ago and said he and Blake were safe but he was afraid to use his cell phone again. A few minutes later, mine went dead during a conversation with my mother. No one's been able to reach Aunt Lydia. That's as much as I know.

That, and my dearest Gina, my guide, my mentor, my friend, is dead. She wants me to do an epilogue. The last thing I wrote was my preface about four months ago and then the notes preceding Aunt Lydia's transcripts, plus a few dozen more edits of the book. We planned nothing else.

Gina, my brilliant Gina, what am I promising to write? How can I do this without you?

I know I'm in danger. So are my mother, my daughter, and probably Aunt Lydia too.

Gina, what do I do?

[Daddy, what do I do?]

19

My Mother's Unanticipated Commentary On Raul's 3,827th Letter

(RL3827C-11051974-TB3)

***

Ed. Note

What follows is Mom's first letter to me from three years ago, the night after Raul's burial. Gina, we both know this was your idea and that I've fought against including "unintended material," but it's getting harder to imagine how this isn't where it was supposed to go all along.

***

January 16, 2017

D*ear Roni,*
I have never written a letter to you. Isn't that strange? I

have been your mother for fifty-seven years and yet not so much as a letter or even an email has ever been exchanged between us.

I wrote so many letters to your father in prison before and just after you were born. They all concerned my feelings about the two of you. But I never mailed any of them. For years they sat in a closed brown shoebox on the top shelf of the living room bookcase. Do you remember it? When I thought you might be old enough to notice, I moved the shoebox to the top shelf of my bedroom closet. The letters came with me when I moved to Lake Shore Drive and are once again sitting on a bookcase shelf. How strange.

Now here I am at 3:45 in the morning, sitting at Lydia's kitchen table in the Bronx just a few hours after we buried your father, and I cannot control the urge to write to you! Isn't that amazing? I know, if I wanted to, I could call you right now and I would probably catch you awake. After what we all experienced and the description of the lights Lydia and Blake saw linking us, I doubt if you are able to sleep either.

Roni, I promised today I would tell you everything. Since I have spent a lifetime telling you almost nothing, that leaves a great deal to tell, and I have been sitting here for the better part of an hour trying to think of where to begin.

Then a few minutes ago I started browsing through your father's letters on the thumb drive you gave me today. What an incredible present! Thank you so much! It was amazing to see his handwriting for the first time and to "hear" him talking to you. I am beginning to understand what you were describing at dinner.

At one point I began dragging the cursor up and down the margin and watched thousands of his letters fly by. Then I just stopped. The letter I stopped on, RL3827, was dated November 5, 1974. In it your father describes what he calls "The First Rule." I don't know if you have run across this letter yet, but I hope you read it the first chance you have. It is brilliant, and written by someone with amazing intellectual and spiritual capacity. I always sensed Raul had this additional depth, this extra dimension and, as different as our backgrounds were, it drew me to him. The voice speaking through that letter is far more sophisticated than the one I remember hearing as a teenager, and yet I recognized it immediately.

Your father's First Rule sounds deceptively simple: "You may not pass along the hurtful things that were passed on to you." He goes on to explain its apparent simplicity could prevent people from taking it seriously and that there needs to be some mechanism for both explaining and implementing the First Rule among the largest possible population.

Can you imagine, Roni, our Raul was sitting in Sing Sing envisioning a mechanism for saving the human race! I cannot even begin to fathom it. And I certainly don't understand the full implications of his Rule. But I feel—yes, that is the only word I can use—I feel what he is saying is absolutely true.

As beautiful as his words are, there is something in the tone of his voice, especially at the end of the letter, that makes me believe he was aware of some difficulty in your life. Perhaps you will be able to remember what it was.

But the most compelling thing for me in his First Rule (actually, in its corollary that he discusses in his next letter) is that we must also pass on the good things that were passed on to us. The more I read those words, the more I think about the crucifix his YouTube video told you to bring today. He seems to have known I would bring my own. I really didn't tell you everything you need to know about the crucifixes, and I think that is where my "everything" needs to start. But first you will need some background.

On the day of my high school graduation, in May of 1957, my father gave another of our parties. This one was for several of my classmates and their parents.

It wasn't that he enjoyed the parties. I think he realized they made your grandmother Anita feel less agitated than she normally did. She might have associated these parties with the ones her family gave when she was little, before she went through a very traumatic experience. I will tell you about it later. Suffice it to say those childhood parties were probably among the few enjoyable memories of her life.

I had graduated from Maria Regina Convent High School that day with highest honors and had been chosen class valedictorian. (I had also graduated at the top of my eighth grade class. Beyond that, I had played my first piano recital when I was seven and was one of only two girls admitted into the University of Puerto Rico pre-med program in 1957—on a full scholarship. Yes, my dear, your brains have a dual pedigree. And I still have my 1956 gold medal for running the fastest 100-yard dash of any girl in the San Juan Diocese!)

I detested these parties, not because I disliked parties but because of what my mother might say or do to embarrass me. By now she was taking an experimental dosage of Thorazine that my father would grind up and attempt to hide in her food, but it was not enough to control her sudden outbursts, especially in front of crowds. Years later at her wake my father told me he believed the life I had lived in Puerto Rico was the one she felt she should have lived. He believed her frustration, coupled with her progressively more delusional state, led her to act out her feelings in progressively stranger ways. What a very sad thing.

I loved being the center of attention, being fawned over and lavishly complimented in environments I could control (which is to say, those my mother could not) and sought out no small number of those environments, all (or most) socially acceptable for a young lady of my upbringing.

Your father was the glaring exception. We met for the first time when I was in third grade at Santo Rosario School in San Juan. Raul was attending fourth grade at the Santo Rosario School Annex our Monsignor had built in a poor area of San

Juan. At the time he was living with his mother and Lydia in a women's shelter.

Each year the main school and the annex would hold a joint eighth grade graduation ceremony in the auditorium of the main school. The annex would send their eighth grade graduates and a contingent of other students, presumably to see and be inspired by how our community lived. At that same ceremony, academic excellence awards were presented to main school students in the lower grades. (Yes, I was a chronic recipient.)

I was walking back to my seat after receiving the third grade general excellence award when I noticed Raul for the first time. Honestly, I have no idea why I looked at him. He was sitting far from the aisle and wearing the same uniform as everyone else. He was also wearing a small, exposed gold crucifix and chain around his neck. For some reason I found myself focusing back and forth between his face and the crucifix.

I had been warned by my mother to stay away from "los telé-fonos." (What color were all telephones in the 1940s and '50s?) Dark-skinned people were bad and did bad things to little girls. Yet, here I was smiling at one of "them." When I got back to my seat, it was obvious from my mother's scowl she had caught it all. She began reprimanding me in an embarrassingly loud whisper, which my father tried to gently hush—as usual, with little success.

Even as her mental state deteriorated, my mother still managed to focus on certain things. She was always concerned about the type of people I might associate with, especially boys. It wasn't that I had any close friends, male or female, and I certainly would have been too embarrassed to bring them to our home. My mother was incapable of focusing on the true source of her problems and compensated by developing a socially acceptable and spontaneously repeated obsession with the presumed sexual ill intentions of anyone with a darker complexion. (Ironically, your Grandfather Hector was olive-skinned, and it is only through a quirk of genetics I was born with a complexion closer to my mother's than to yours.)

I saw Raul at a few more grammar school functions and always felt that same attraction. Then he was gone, and for several years there was no contact of any kind.

At some point toward the end of my junior year at Maria Regina he reappeared. I remember, he was standing outside the schoolyard fence one day, and he just smiled when I spotted him. Oh, he was such a handsome young man!

In those days my mother insisted I be driven to and from school. After a while I worked out an arrangement with my driver. He would drop me at a park three blocks from my school, where Raul would be waiting. We would spend no more than ten minutes together, and the driver would blame our delay on traffic.

The first time your father and I were alone in the park, we just looked into each other's eyes and smiled. I lifted his crucifix, the same one, and kissed it. He did the same with my crucifix. The next thing I knew, we were kissing. It was our first and still the most beautiful kiss I can ever remember.

Our park meetings continued regularly for a couple of months, but they were all in public and I was always fearful of being seen by someone who could identify me. Then one day, out of the blue, my mother accused me of seeing a "Black boy." Of course, I denied it vehemently, and after a few days she dropped the matter. I wasn't sure if she had fantasized it all but, just to be safe, I began to severely limit my time with Raul. That made me detest my mother all the more.

Around that same time, the neighbors on the other side of our back yard wall moved and left their house vacant. They had begun to build their house just a couple of years after we moved into ours. Even before it was finished, I remember my mother insisting my father construct a stone wall between our two properties. When the zoning regulations limited its height to four feet, she further insisted he plant every kind of palm tree and shrub to block the neighbors' view.

Our neighbors eventually retaliated by building a large tool shed behind their house, nearly flush against "Hadrian's Wall." Now it offered me a daring opportunity. I told Raul to meet me in the empty shed. He would have to carry a large laborer's garden fork (which I "borrowed" from our shed) so he would not draw attention in our neighborhood and make sure he approached by a route that was not visible from our house. I would simply go for one of my walks and casually detour to the unoccupied property.

Raul was waiting for me in the shed when I arrived. I took perverse pleasure in poking my head around the corner and peering over the wall and through the flora at our back veranda. My mother was sprawled on a chaise longue about fifty yards from the wall, sipping a lemonade and jabbering away to nobody.

We made love for the first time, standing up, as I leaned back against one of the shed walls. Raul was so gentle. I can still feel his hands and his lips and every part of him. (I'll bet you never thought you'd hear those words from your mother! I never thought I would ever think them again, much less write them, but, Roni, I promised you everything.)

Our regular plan was for Raul to wait for five minutes after I left the shed, dirty his hands and his garden fork, then stroll out of the neighborhood at an inconspicuous pace. I would race home at full speed by some circuitous route sporting the world's broadest smile.

After several of these liaisons Juanita, our maid, put two and two together. I begged her not to say anything to my mother. She went a step further and helped me plan out the best times to meet with Raul. Thinking back, I don't think I could have survived in that house without Juanita. I lost all contact with her after we left San Juan.

Raul and I were once again in the shed as my high school graduation party was getting under way. Although that afternoon would have been the worst possible time for us to meet, he had insisted on seeing me, and I was very concerned. A few weeks earlier, he had hinted he and his mother might move to New York City. It had already become a mecca for poor Puerto Ricans and his aunt (Lydia) was looking for an apartment for them in an area he called the "wes sigh." My fear was he was going to announce their imminent departure, and I was right.

Several times while we made love, my mother shouted for me to come down from my room to meet my guests. It was unnerving and made our liaison the most intense I can ever remember. We were both rushing to get dressed when he broke the news. I could not look into his eyes after he told me, as if not looking would make it all go away.

He took my hand and gently kissed it. Then, just as gently, he removed his crucifix and chain, placed them in my hand, and softly folded my fingers over them. Roni, you learned a few hours ago that was the same crucifix and chain Lydia had gotten from her mother and then placed around Raul's neck the day he was born. I removed my own crucifix and chain and folded his fingers over them the same way.

Then he was gone. I ran home by one of my usual routes crying my eyes out the whole time. Juanita was expecting me and quickly ushered me up the servants' staircase. It took me, maybe, two minutes to clear my eyes, change my clothes, and freshen my makeup. I made my grand entrance and for the remainder of the day acted like the perfect princess I was expected to be, even as my heart was breaking.

That was in May of 1957. By September we had moved to New York City for reasons I did not quite understand at the time and, amazingly, wound up on the same block as Raul and Lydia. My father knew my mother would soon need institutionalization and that Puerto Rico did not have the best facilities. Moreover, it would be impossible to keep her institutionalization a secret. New York City, on the other hand, had some of the best psychiatric facilities in the country and was sixteen hundred miles from home.

The apartment building we moved into on West 64th Street between 9th and 10th Avenues was to be torn down in less than two years to make way for Lincoln Center. In the meanwhile, landlords were offering cheap, month-to-month rents as the neighborhood began to empty out. The population was largely Puerto Rican, and my father figured it offered the best temporary financial arrangement for him and a tolerable cultural arrangement for my mother. I was never consulted about the move. Even if I had been, my mother's undisclosed needs most certainly would have trumped any objections I might have had.

Not long before we left San Juan, my father abruptly quit his job as executive vice president at Traducciones Profesionales, the largest business document translation company in Latin America, even knowing he was the anointed successor to the retiring CEO. He sold everything he had very quickly and secretly and at a severe loss, so much so that he found himself a few dollars short of the cash price of one of the new row houses they were building in Castle

Hill. (It is the one I am sitting in right now. He willed it to your Aunt Lydia.) He calculated it would take him about eighteen months to pull together the remainder working at the only job he could find in New York City, a lower middle-management document translation position with newly opened Goya Foods in Brooklyn.

Thinking back, there are so many better ways he could have handled the situation. Any one of his friends in the finance industry could have helped him preserve the vast majority of his assets. But he was sworn to secrecy about everything involving my mother, and it was his compulsive need to maintain that secrecy that, regrettably, drove him to do things in the least reasonable and, ultimately, the most costly way.

Still, his actions helped bring us to where we are today.

I had no idea you would be bringing my crucifix and chain to Raul's burial, much less that you would be doing so at Raul's request. Somehow he knew I would bring his. And somehow he had to know what would happen when it was all passed on to you and Blake.

Roni, I do not pretend to understand what happened today. All I know is that it was one of the most beautiful days of my life and that Raul made it happen, even as we were burying him.

How can this be?

I Love You, Roni.

Mom

20

AUNT LYDIA'S VIDEO COMMENTARIES ON EVERYTHING—PART 2

(RL1C-05141964-LF3-2)

Mirona: Aunt Lydia, when we started, you said your father turned the brothel into a school you attended. Did I get that right?

Lydia: Yeah! That's what he done.

Mirona: (extended silence) Soooo ... how do you turn a brothel ...

Lydia: (laughs, over Mirona) Heh! You so *easy*! ... (group laughter) OK, OK. (sighs) I told you, me and my mother get kicked outta the house by the pimp, OK? So I'm livin' in the shelter with Sister Paolo and some women and some little kids.

And Celia was there too … after the pimp (slashing gesture) cut her face, 'cause … she couldn't work no more and she was, eh … *embarazada* (pregnant) … with Raul.

So one day, Sister Paolo tell us we need some more money, you know, for food and stuff like dat. And she don't know how she gonna *get* it. And me, I'm thinkin', you know … *how?* And I look at Celia … and then I get this idea, you know? And she already pretty *big*. So I get one of the dresses she use to work in. I mean, it was *tight! Ev'*rything (shakes one hand under breasts, one under belly) all *over* the place!

So … (chuckles) So I go out in the street, in fronna the house, and I'm waiting for the men to come out. You know … I *know* all these guys. They come all the time when I was runnin' the place. And … a lot come for Celia and they pay me more for her 'cause, you know, she was really *pret*ty.

So when they come out, I walk up to them. And Celia hidin' across the street. They don't see her. And I say to them, "Hi, how ya doin'?" And they surprise, 'cause, you know … they ain't *seen* me for a while. And then I say (chuckles) … I say, "You wanna say hello to Celia?" And then (chuckles) … I point to Celia, and she come out, and she smile and she done like *this* (rubs her belly) … *reeeeal* slow! And the men … heh! They … they jus' *look*in' at her with the *mouth* open, and … and the *eyes* poppin' out! (group chuckles)

And then I say to them, (imploringly) "You know, Celia need a little help, you know, with the baby? You think? … maybe? … you know?" An' *every one* of them! They pull out the *wallet* and they givin' me all *kinds* of money. And they sayin', (mock fear) "Please, don't tell my wife!" "Don't tell my *girl*friend!" (group laughs)

We done that all afternoon ... and all night. And we got ... I remember ... (pointing, slowly) three hundred and twenny-six dollars. (elevates) *Three hun*dred and ...You know how much that was then? *Shit*, that was a *lot*ta money!

And I give it all to Sister. And then she give me ... seventy-five dollars. Nine-year-old kid. *Seventy-five do*llars! Uhm! ... And I take some of the money, and I buy a nice dress for Celia. (gestures) You know, to cover the baby.

Mirona: (pause) I don't know where to ... (pause) You said you were running a brothel ... at nine years old?

Lydia: No. (pause, remembers) No, I start when I was eight.

Mirona: (incredulous) How?

Lydia: (shrugs, scoffing) How? I ... I just *done* it! I take the money from the men, and every day I give the pimp what he s'pose to get. (pointing, forcefully) And I *never* cheat! And then I pay *La Hara* (the police). And if I seen the wrong lights, I tell the girl, "Don't do this one." And they *lis*-sen to me ... (pause, reflects) pretty much. And I cook for my mother and me. But ... when she was high? ... she don't eat so much, so ...

Mirona: But how did your father turn the brothel into a school?

Lydia: OK. So ... after I done that with Celia, you know, a lotta the men don't come *back* no more. They was afraid someone gonna *tell.* So now the pimp … (gestures) he ain't makin' no *money.* So when the Bishop send the men to ask him if he wanna sell the place, he had to say *yes.* But they don't pay him hardly *noth*in'.

Mirona: Wait a minute. What men are we talking about?

Lydia: (comic reprimand) There's a lot goin' on here, Mirona. You try to keep up, OK? (group laughter).

Mirona: (sarcastic exasperation) God knows I …

Lydia: (over her) Now … (gestures) OK, first I gotta go back. One day, I went to the *big* school, the *real* school, Santo Rosario, 'cause I wanna see a priest … 'cause I just kill this guy who was tryin' to kill my mother in the house. *Crazy* guy. With a *Bi*ble or somethin'. And they a'ways say … you know, you s'pose to see a *priest.*

Mirona: *How* old were you?

Lydia: I *told* you! I was, like … nine.

Mirona: (long pause, resigned) OK.

Lydia: And I was wearin' my u-nee-form, same one like the kids in the *big* school, 'cause Sister Paolo already ask my father if we can have a small school in the *shel*ter. And he say *yes,* but only 'cause Sister figure out he's my *real* father. So … he don't want no trouble from her, you know? And …

Mirona: (interrupting) How did she find …?

Lydia: (over her) Wai', wai', wai'! You gonna hear the whole story. Jus' … (pause) So I go upstairs to his office … with my father. And it's *big!* Lotsa statues and chairs and pictures. And he tryin' to talk to me like he don't know who I *am*. But then I look at him … and I *see*! He got the *lights* … just like *me*. And … and then I seen this kinda light that means … (emotionally) he's my *real* father! … And he sees it *too*!

And I got so *angry* at him. I mean … all my *life*! He knows who I am. And he just … leave me in the house … and then the shelter … after he done it with my mother … in the house. (pause, resigned) But he's a priest, so … what's he gonna *do*, you know?

Now … they was this nun, young kid, maybe … nineteen, twenny? … and she seen the lights in *me* … *and* him! I know. 'Cause … I can *see*. And she got so *angry* at him because the Monsignor run *ev*erything, and the nuns gotta do whatever he say.

And now he got a *kid*? Heh! So she write a letter to, uh … to … uhhh … (off mike) *Teresa, como se llama el Cardinal?* (Teresa, what was the Cardinal's name?)

Teresa: (off mike) She wrote a letter to Archbishop Spellman here in New York. He hadn't been made a Cardinal yet, but he was a close confidant of the new Pope, Pius the twelfth. And Spellman was considered one of the top power brokers in the American church.

Lydia: Yeah. So she write to him and she thinkin', "I'm gonna *nail* this guy! He de*serve* it!" But (chuckles) wha' happen was … Heh! … *Spell*-mun? He get angry at *her*! 'Cause the nuns ain't suppose to *say* nothin'.

Then … he turn aroun' and he tell my father's boss, the Bishop, to make a new school … for the poor kids jus' so no one gonna

... you know, *think* about it too much. If my father around *all* the poor kids, nobody gonna look at *him* ... and then look at *me*, and figure it out ... (points) the *eyes*, you know? Smart! 'Cause if somebody find out what *really* happen ... it don' look so good for the *Bi*shop! (pause) *Or* the Pope.

Mirona: (softly) Hmm ... plain sight ... (pause, shift) What happened to that young nun?

Lydia: My father told me. The Bishop send her off to some ... some *mission* ... in the jungle ... in *El Salvador*. Gone.

Mirona: (long pause) Could Sister Paolo see the lights?

Lydia: No. (taps chest with two hands, closes eyes) No, she had these *beauty*-ful lights comin' down to her, and comin' outta her but ... No, she couldn' see them. (elevates) My *moth*er could see the lights! But she stop seein' them when I was ... yeah, when the pimp kick us outta the house and she go with Jesús. (pause, softly) Uhm!

So the Bishop, he know what my father done but he don' wanna *say* nothin'. Gotta keep it *quiet*, you know? So he send these men out to buy the house from the *pimp* ... and he *buy* it. *Real* cheap. And then he tell my father, "You gonna make this into a school for the poor kids. And you gonna make a *big* deal about it." You know, newspaper, and on the radio and all that stuff. And he know, this gonna make my father ... *muy nervioso* (very nervous) but ... (chuckle) that's what he wanna *do*! That's how they *do* t'ings ... these people.

Mirona: But … how did the Monsignor … I mean, how did Sister Paolo know the Monsignor was your father?

Lydia: Ah! OK. So … when I was a little girl, my mother give me these two books. With pictures. One teach you how to count the numbers and the other teach you how to read … you know, *ea*sy words. So … I read the books and I *teach* myself. That … Tha's how I know how much money to give the pimp every night. I learn. By myself.

So one day Sister ask to look at my books. And I give them to her and … she lookin' at all the pages and … and then she open the front of the book. And on the inside of the, uh … uh … the *cov*er they got this piece of paper. And the paper say, (carefully) "Property of Santo Rosario School." And when I was little, I couldn' read that.

So then Sister say to me, "Where you get these *books*?" And I tell her, "From my *moth*er." And soon I say that … she lookin' *right* in my eyes. You know, same color like my father. Nobody got eyes like that. (secretively) And she don't say nothin' … But she knew. *Right* there. She knew. (long silence)

Blake: (looks at her cell phone, off mike) Oh, shit! I've gotta go …

Gina: Did you get some ideas for …

Blake: (over her, chuckling) *So* many! But I told Matthew I'd do the next edit on the archetype segment before the end of the day. I … I've really gotta go.

Gina: It's OK. Just tell him you were with me.

Blake: (uncomfortably) I know, but … I don't wanna …

Gina: It's OK, Blake. Just tell Matthew to call me after seven.

Blake: I will. Bye, Mom. (chair moving, kisses, fast steps)

Mirona/Lydia: Bye, Beebs / *Blakita.* (door opens/closes)

Lydia: (long pause) You know, sometime I wish she still had the blue hair. (light chuckles).

Mirona: (pensive pause) She's changed.

Gina: (smiling pause, kindly) So has her mother.

21

RAUL'S 5,644TH LETTER

(RL5644-10271979)

Dear Mirona,

First, I want to apologize for not writing to you yesterday. You know I promised I would and that I have never broken my promise before. You also know I don't talk about many of the things that happen here, but it is important that you know about yesterday.

It started out like most other days. I meditated for about a half hour before breakfast, then went back to continue work on the syllabus for the new "Introduction to Philosophy" course we have been developing. (You would be surprised how many people are signing up to take it.) I taught my ten o'clock English class and, rather than correct papers as I normally would, I decided I would go out into the exercise yard for the end of the morning session. I am not much of an athlete, but I enjoy having conversations with my students as I walk.

For as long as I have been here, men have always tended to congregate or form friendships along racial lines. This is just an extension of how they socialized on the outside and is usually of little consequence. Occasionally, however, racially defined groups expand and develop into something resembling a gang. Gang membership offers a kind of solace and a sense of protection, especially for newer arrivals. You and I have talked about the need to feel protected many times. It is the same need that drew me to Los Diablos Latinos (The Latin Devils).

The guards keep a close watch on potential gang structures and can usually prevent the worst types of initiation activities or potential conflicts with rival groups. But over the past several months there has been a particularly large influx of new men, Black, White, and Latino, many with strong prior gang affiliations. Two men in particular, one Black and one White, had been leaders of very large gangs and had fought each other on several occasions in the past.

The guards somehow failed to make the connections and housed both men in my block. Within days each had organized a new rival gang. The authorities only realized what was happening when a fight broke out in the dining hall. This was about four months ago. The gang leaders were immediately removed to different blocks and many of the members were isolated. Things appeared to calm down, but both gangs continued to quietly recruit and expand.

I sensed a rise in tensions of late but did not appreciate just how rapidly they were rising. Today while I was walking with Desmond, several people on the opposite side of the yard began to shout. That must have been a signal because, seconds later, shivs (improvised knives) were drawn and men were fighting hand-to-hand all around us.

Suddenly, I was confronted by a White man who called me a SPIC and lunged at me with his weapon. Desmond grabbed his arm at the last instant, wrestled his weapon away, and kneed him in the stomach.

As the White man went down, a Black man, one of my former students, came rushing at Desmond screaming, "Mon-key." It is a derogatory term used by American Blacks to demean Caribbean Blacks. Before Desmond could react, my ex-student had stabbed him in the heart. Desmond collapsed right on top of the White man.

That left me and my former student staring at one another. I knew in that instant he did not want to kill me but that sparing me would put his own life in jeopardy.

Mirona, you know how powerful and empowering soulful knowing can be. At that instant the Infinite Transcendence aligned with my subconscious and I was empowered to straighten up, smile at my ex-student, and then turn my left shoulder toward him. I waited for what could not have been more than one or two seconds. Suddenly my ex-student screamed, "SPIC," and lunged at me. He could have stabbed me in the heart as well, but I already knew he could not and would not. He redirected his shiv upward and stabbed me through my left shoulder muscle.

An instant later he was shot in the back by one of the guards and fell dead at my feet. Then a number of other shots were fired from various points in the yard. Within seconds the fighting ended and men were racing toward the yard walls.

All that was left in the middle of the yard was the guard who shot my ex-student, a moaning White man, one dead Black American, one dead Black from the Caribbean, and me. I looked around and saw at least twenty guards with drawn weapons pointed at men huddled against the walls. On the ground, scattered among the guards, were at least a dozen dead or severely wounded inmates. I sensed several Souls departing bodies.

The entire prison was placed on lockdown. I was able to walk to the infirmary on my own. Before the afternoon was out, at least fifteen more men had been admitted.

After I received stitches and was bandaged up, I requested a pencil and paper to write your letter. My right arm, my writing arm, was perfectly fine and I could have easily written it. But the doctors and orderlies were too busy caring for the badly wounded to deal with my request. They kept me overnight to make sure no infection set in and released me this morning.

The population in my block has been significantly altered. There are no more gang members here, at least none I am aware of. Presumably, the key surviving belligerents have all been placed in solitary confinement. If the usual protocols are followed, some of them will eventually be relocated to different blocks and others to different institutions altogether. Many will face new criminal trials. Fortunately, all of my current students are still in the block.

Except, of course, for Desmond. Please, Mirona, when you have the chance, meditate peacefully on the state of his soul and its eventual transition. I can tell you he is being attracted to a better existence and I am very happy for him. Of course, I don't know where, when, or in what dimension that existence will take place, but I do know it will be far more peaceful than his most recent incarnation.

Still, I am pained by the suffering he experienced during his most recent life and especially at the last moment of that life, and I will miss him dearly as a friend. Please honor his memory when you can.

It will not surprise you to know I had a very vivid dream last night. This is what always happens when the subconscious is so strongly stimulated. But even I was surprised at how intense and how detailed my dream was. It involved you in a wonderful way, sweetheart, and I want you to know about it.

The dream is an almost perfect reenactment of what you and I have defined as my energetic epiphany, the night after your moth-

er's visit. It begins with her racing out of the visiting room in tears. I cannot see her face, but when I look down at the floor behind her chair, I see your five-year-old picture. It is not quite the same picture your mother brought with her that day. In that picture you had a squinting smile on your face. In this picture you are crying. In fact, the picture is animated and I can hear you crying as well.

The dream shifts to my cell. It is nearly pitch-black. I am on my knees with my back to the cell bars. Tied around my neck is one end of a thin piece of silk thread. The other end of the thread is tied to the prison bars. This, again, is different from what actually happened that night. As you know, I was contemplating suicide and was in the same physical position, except it was the cotton cord from my pajama bottoms that connected my neck to the bars.

Then, in the dream, I lean forward, just as I did that night. But instead of me backing up and starting to cry, the silk thread just passes right through my neck. After that, I experience the same three images that passed through my mind that night once I decided to continue living. The first is your picture on the floor again, except in the dream I see you as I know you are now, a beautiful twenty-one-year-old woman. You have a lovely smile on your face but, in a matter of seconds, it begins to fade and, seconds after that, you begin to cry just like your five-year-old self.

The second and third images are exactly the same as they were that night. In the second, I am standing in the middle of 64th

Street with the barrel of a gun in my mouth. Suddenly, I look up and see Lydia scream my name from her window. I can't hear her, but I see her lips forming my name.

In the third image, I watch the outside of my left cheek as a smooth shining object passes through it in slow motion without breaking the skin or drawing any blood. When the object is several inches away, it suddenly explodes with a deafening sound.

That night, I was once again aware of myself kneeling on the floor of my cell. I began to cry silently. Gradually, as a profound calmness came over me, I stopped crying and slowly removed my pajama bottoms cord from both my neck and the bars.

My dream was a bit different. I don't cry. And the sense of calm is already within me. I touch my neck and realize there is nothing attaching me to the bars.

That night, the moment I disconnected myself from the bars, I had this intense image of what I once described to you as electrical connections extending from Lydia in her bed to me in my cell, and then from the two of us to you in the bed where you were sleeping in Lydia's house.

In the dream, I watch a beam of silver light descend through the top of my cell and surround my head and neck. I look up and can see the beam coming from far above. I drift upward and begin following it back to its source.

The beam passes through the roof of the prison, then rises to a height of perhaps three hundred feet and begins to track south-

ward over the Hudson River. The night is crystal clear and the sky is filled with stars. Looking down, I can see the beam's beautiful silver reflection on the motionless surface of the water. I have never flown over the Hudson River but I seem to recognize landmarks on either side of it.

Now I am I focusing on a rotating beacon flashing alternating red and white beams from the top of the east pier of the George Washington Bridge, about five miles ahead. As I reach the bridge, the silver light veers to the left and I begin following it through different neighborhoods in the Bronx.

Finally the beam descends through the roof of an attached house I have never seen before, but I know it is Lydia's. The beam terminates on Lydia's chest. She is just lying in bed and looks at me with a peaceful expression. Then she points to the wall behind her bed.

I pass through the wall and find myself in an adjoining bedroom with two twin beds. Your mother is asleep on one of them. She is curled up tightly and has nearly covered her head with her blanket.

You are lying face up and asleep on the other bed and are having what appears to be a bad dream. Occasionally you moan or stir slightly. As I focus on you in the dark, I am aware that you are all the ages you have ever been and will ever be.

At that same moment I become aware a different beam of silver light has followed me into the bedroom. The edge of the beam is resting between my shoulder blades. Slowly, it passes through my heart and then envelops you. At that same moment a narrower beam of light extends from my pubic region and blends with the first beam.

A calmness comes over you, and your five-year-old self smiles. As you do, I feel a love and a connection with you I have never felt with another human being.

Then the light lets me know I need to follow it once again. As I rise through Lydia's roof, I realize there are actually two parallel beams of light: the one that came from Lydia to me in my cell and the one that I brought with me on my journey.

The lights lead me directly back to my cell. Once again, I am standing there feeling perfectly calm. I look up and see the beams departing through the roof above me. Then I awake.

That first night, once the calmness had descended on me, I went to my desk, searched in the dark for a piece of paper, and wrote the words "Dear Mirona" for the first time.

As I said, I have never felt closer to a human being than I felt to you that night. And I have never lost that feeling. Not even a part of it and not even for an instant. Ever. Sweetheart, I am always, always with you. Nothing will ever change that. Ever.

I will write to you again tomorrow.

I love you, sweetheart.

Kisses,

Daddy

22

EDITOR'S COMMENTARY ON RAUL'S 5,644TH LETTER

(RL5644C-10271979-MG1)

I can't read this letter without tearing up, not the first time I read it or any time since.

Tear trigger number one is right up front when my father says he's missed a day of writing to me. As I was reading through his letters the first time, I kept trying to deny how attached I was becoming, and I still have a problem with it, but the first time I realized there'd been even the slightest break in his daily contacts, it literally scared the shit out of me.

Raul's descriptions of prison violence in RL5644 are the most graphic of all his prison descriptions. But I don't think he was trying to sensationalize prison life or frighten me any more than I already was the day he wrote this letter.

What I think [what I hope] he was saying was, even here, even under these wretched conditions, you can depend on me unconditionally. I've made an unbreakable commitment. I'm with you and will be with you and will guide you every moment of your life, no matter how absurd the circumstances of your life at that moment, no matter how detestable the behavior or how poor the choices that occasioned those circumstances, even when there's no life left in my body. Even if I missed a day.

Before I can back out of the feelings completely, I always manage to think of Alan.

I met Alan Schneider during my freshman year at Columbia. We were both declared business majors and taking several of the same prerequisite courses. He seemed smart enough to be at Columbia, but just about average in most other ways. I would've never considered him worthy of my attention if it hadn't been for the events of one particularly outrageous evening just before Christmas break that first year.

Living on the upper west side of Manhattan was a liberating experience. Here I could act out almost any outrageous thing I could imagine [most of that acting out facilitated by alcohol and occasionally enhanced by some contraband substance]. Somehow I managed to maintain excellent grades even as party time came close to exceeding class and study time combined.

The racial issue I'd pushed off against in Chicago wasn't nearly as pronounced in this part of the city. And the very idea of a posse was *so* high school.

So who shall I be? After weighing all available options, I settled on Clint Eastwood in a miniskirt. That meant I had no real friends, but everyone had to know who I was, and a great many people wanted to know who I really was. They'd start light conversations and attempt to negotiate the Roni maze. Their glaring insecurities gave me a rush and I got off even more on misdirecting their efforts.

Men, from undergrads to full professors, wanted me. I was hot, smart, an enigma, the forbidden other, and radiated the perception of power. I was also convinced I could have any man I wanted but was careful to focus only on those who, I calculated, would be fully responsive.

One night that December I overheard some girls in my dorm whispering that my roommate's boyfriend, a Columbia junior, was "*super!*" hot. My roommate that first semester was this annoyingly blonde trust-fund baby [Barb!] who ceaselessly let it be known her [much poorer] boyfriend was absolutely faithful to her. I'd already calculated I could have him. Now it became a challenge.

I made a bet with one of the more clueless whisperers. I would screw Barb's boyfriend and present the proof, and if I did, she'd do my laundry for the next two months. The little jerk asked what she'd get if I failed: "Nothing, of course."

The West End was this old Victorian bar directly across Broadway at 114th Street and had been the haunt of people like Jack Kerouac and William Burroughs. In those days the drinking age was still eighteen, and even though my eighteenth birthday was still a little ways off, it was understood all Columbia students got served.

The bigger issue was a school rule that first-semester freshmen weren't allowed to drink at the local bars. The rule was rarely enforced, but when it was, the penalty could be as severe as expulsion.

I spotted her boyfriend, Evan, standing at the bar and positioned myself so he'd notice. Not long afterward he worked his way over with two beers. He obviously knew who I was and made some crack about freshmen drinkers. I held steady eye contact and responded with something like, "Who said I was here to drink?"

Fifteen minutes later we were screwing in one of the men's room stalls. Evan was wearing these dumb, shamrock-covered boxers— which I breathlessly requested as a souvenir.

By the time I got back to the dorm, Barb had left for Old Greenwich. That left me the whole weekend to figure out how to plant the boxers so she'd find them without making it look obvious. I decided to leave just a hint of shamrock sticking out of my bottom dresser drawer. Barb was a neat freak and constantly adjusting things, hers and mine. She wouldn't be able to resist.

That Sunday night about an hour after she returned to campus, Barb beat the hell out of Evan on the steps of the administration building. I watched it all from a safe distance with my new launderette. His parting "Fuck you ... *Bitch*!" sounded like something he'd wanted to tell her for quite some time. Barb never spoke another word to me.

About a week later, the day our Christmas break began, I found the edge of a note sticking out of my bottom dresser drawer. Barb was dropping out of Columbia, it was entirely my fault, and I'd be foolish to assume there'd be no repercussions.

There was also a letter from the university in my mailbox. I was to appear at a hearing when classes resumed to answer allegations about drinking at the West End. What I hadn't known until then was that Barb's father was a former Colombia trustee and maintained close ties with several current trustees.

Given my nonrelationship with my mother, I'd planned on spending the Christmas break in a dorm set aside for people like me while the other dorms were being cleansed. It so happened Alan Schneider was staying in the same dorm. His mother was off cavorting in Europe, and he had no real relationship with his father.

Over the next few days I racked my brains for the best plan of action. I didn't even notice Alan. Then, one afternoon, he just walked up to me and with no discernible agenda asked what was wrong. He asked as though we'd known each other our entire lives. I tried to find a reason not to respond but couldn't. The entire story just spilled out of me in semi-truthful form while Alan just listened.

Then I started talking about Chicago and my mother and a shitload of other things. And as I went along, I noticed my information was becoming more accurate. Alan kept listening.

Finally he said, "Let me cover for you." Never in my life had I heard those words from another human. He laid out this scenario that had the two of us bumping into each other on campus that Friday night fifteen minutes after I went to the West End, at Barb's request, to tell Evan she was upset and wanted to see him before she left for the weekend. No, I wasn't drinking but, yes, I did enter the West End, at which point I was offered a drink I did not consume. I have no idea who bought it for me and left the bar immediately after conveying my message. I was deeply concerned about the appearance of breaking a school regulation, especially as a full scholarship student, and poured my heart out to Alan.

It was brilliant. Given the normal level of chaos at the West End on a Friday night and its lack of sober witnesses, coupled with the virtual absence of witnesses in the dorms, it was an entirely plausible story and one that would be difficult to disprove. I would threaten/save/own Evan's ass [Alan correctly calculated Evan would never admit to buying drinks for a freshman] and would force Barb to return to campus to admit to her personal humiliation and the very public beating she'd administered if she wanted to pursue the matter.

I presented the story to a three-man hearing panel about two weeks later. Alan was asked to appear separately. Our stories were in total synch, and we never heard a word back from anyone. If either presentation had been anything less than perfect, I'm convinced we would have both been expelled.

For me, colluding with another human was beyond unimaginable. Collusion meant revealing secrets and an unavoidable level of trust. Both were foreign concepts. I was *Roni Pod*, the superior, the desirable, the presumed dangerous, and above all else, the unknowable. Now Alan knew more about me than anyone ever had, including my mother, and he hadn't even solicited the information.

I spent the first few days after the hearing calculating the best way to deal with him. Normally I would have trusted my first instinct to avoid him completely, but I found myself challenging that instinct almost immediately. I mean, if Alan was the type of person even Roni Pod could confide in about her predicament, why shouldn't she be in contact with him now?

Ah, but Roni Pod didn't *really* confide in anyone. So it all had to be part of some super-convoluted deal. Yeah, that was it. And if I could simply come up with the necessary quid pro quo to finally close out that deal, I could go right on being whoever I thought I needed to be.

After one of our classes, I approached him. My plan was to say, "Tell me what you want …" in the way only Roni Pod could say it. He'd stammer something about wanting to screw me, and nature would take its course.

But as I delivered my one-liner, to my utter horror, I heard Roni Pod starting to stammer. She couldn't just dismiss the upset victory our team had pulled off. Alan sensed my dilemma [he did, really] and smiled. Then, ignoring it altogether, he asked if I'd like to go with him to the Café Continental in Forest Hills, a one-hour, multi-subway ride from the campus. It was a bar-restaurant near one of his father's homes that catered to Eastern European types. He said it was a riot to watch guys in dark pinstriped suits and wrong ties try to pick up the type of women who trolled for them while this ancient trio played perfectly marinated background music on Friday nights.

I loved the idea. Alan already knew my real history. Without saying it, we had both decided it would be a pisser to go make fun of my phony one.

I pretended to be by myself. Alan sat two stools away. When some pinstriped guy finally approached me, I morphed into Ludmila Podlovskya from Azerbaijan complete with the world's thickest, Russo-Eastern-Europeanish accent. I came from an unpronounceable village where they spoke only an obscure dialect; picked up a few English words from the occasional Voice of America broadcast; recently disembarked from a tramp steamer at the Port of Newark; and, only today, found employment (*Iz zo lowkee!*) as a dumpling edger at a Brooklyn pierogi factory. (Oh, and eighteen years ago my mother dropped in unexpectedly on some distant male cousin in Marrakesh.)

I kept a totally incomprehensible conversation going with this guy, in character, for fifteen straight minutes. Alan was convulsed with stifled laughter. The guy never got it. After resurrecting every language and every obscure dialect he'd ever known to get through to me, he finally blurted out an unmistakable curse that unmistakably analogized cow and woman, and just stormed out.

Alan moved over and I began laughing like I'd never laughed in my entire life. [Really.] Alan too. Tears were streaming down our cheeks. I gave him this exceedingly long, laughing hug and proceeded to get exceptionally drunk.

Over the next four years I led a double life of sorts. I was Roni Pod to everyone but Alan. To him I was *Loody* when no one else was in earshot.

Alan saved Loody's ass. Regularly. Nearly all savings involved getting her the hell out of some wrong bar after she'd mouthed off to some wrong person. I felt safe with him around and would fuck up in ways Roni Pod never could.

Loody even felt safe enough to scream at and, I'm not proud to say, hit Alan when hitting and screaming were the only way she could act out whatever it was she couldn't disgorge. Alan took it all as he tried talking sense to the increasingly senseless.

During one of my more drunken/impassioned, hitting/ screaming sessions [he told me], I suddenly froze, then began trying to kiss him passionately. We were on the Belt Parkway near Coney Island in his ancient TR4, and as I threw myself at him the second time, I managed to yank the wheel completely out of his hands, forcing us onto the Cropsey Avenue exit ramp. Somehow Alan regained control of the car (and me), pulled over, and spent the next ten minutes trying to keep me from taking my top off. Then [he told me] I politely passed out and we proceeded not to have sex again.

On October 27, 1979, the date of my father's letter, I was once again with Alan in his TR4. We were first-year MBA students at Columbia, both on full scholarships, and I was at my apex of alcohol consumption [at that stage of my life]. It was getting harder even for me to tell Roni Pod and Loody apart.

The day before, Alan's mother had called from somewhere in France to announce he'd collected yet another stepfather. Her latest foray into legitimate coupling had apparently been prompted by the Brazilian remarriage of Alan's father just two weeks before that. I'd already concluded his parents were both thoughtless asses who were using him in an incredibly immature way. They'd telephone him to bitch and moan about each other. Alan would listen and, of course, offer eminently reasonable advice. [I couldn't imagine I'd be bitching and moaning to my own daughter pretty much the same way long after my marriage to her father had nosedived to a vicious end.]

It was Alan's idea to drive to Provincetown on Cape Cod that Saturday. His father, who was still on his honeymoon, kept an office-apartment in Boston, about an hour off the Cape, and we planned to stay there that night.

He was unusually quiet during the ride out, and I drew the obvious connection between this and the weddings. Still, we had an unspoken arrangement. Alan must do everything necessary to prop up Loody, and she could tolerate just so much slacking off. I remember trying to cheer him up during the drive. After a while, I was giving pep talks, and by the time we hit the Sagamore Bridge

I was browbeating him. Alan kept trying to reassert his supportive persona, but his heart wasn't in it.

An hour or so later we were settled in at the Crown & Anchor on Commercial Street. He seemed pleasant enough, but the drinks were going down at an abnormally fast clip. Alan had this amazing capacity for alcohol and I'd never actually seen him drunk, but as time went on I realized he was committed to getting piss-faced, and it bothered the hell out of me.

For a while I matched him drink for drink until I realized the familiar Alan was no longer sitting next to me. As he went to take his next slug, I held his wrist to the bar, and not gently. It was the first time I'd ever tried to stop Alan from doing anything.

He made no eye contact. Then he started to smile something like Alan, but froze up at pre-grimace. Finally, softly: "Let go of me." I wouldn't. He looked at me, flatly, like Roni Pod might have: "I said … let go."

This was a stranger. This was not the Alan who tended to Loody. This person was gravely wounded, and neither Loody nor Roni Pod had the tools, the capacity or, frankly, the interest to deal with his injuries. I released his wrist and stared at him as he slugged down his drink. Then I tipped over what was left of my own and stormed out of the bar. For the first time ever, Alan didn't come after me.

That left me level-two buzzed and alone on Commercial Street in the salt-air dusk with more locals than tourists on a cool, late

October evening. Provincetown does not lack for bars, and I quickly found another one.

About two drinks later a large, bull dykish woman plopped herself down on the stool next to me. I'd seen her at the Crown & Anchor [bull dyke central during high season] and thought I'd given off all the necessary "do not attempt" signals. [Under P-town rules, storming away from a man instantly reversed their polarity.]

She started right in with the Honey-I-know-what-you're-going-through bit. I was in no mood and tried to ignore her. But when she gently placed her hand on my wrist, something in my brain exploded.

The next thing I knew, I was on my feet shoving her off her stool and cursing her with every ounce of my strength. It took her a few seconds to regain her bearings from ground level.

Then a wild beast lunged for my leg. I kicked it someplace, raced out of the bar, and sprinted for the Crown & Anchor screaming Alan's name the whole way. The whole place must have heard me coming. Everyone was on their feet, including Alan. I'd barely made it through the front door when Miss Dyke put me in a chokehold from behind.

I can remember Alan racing toward me. [Those next few seconds have always been a blur.] Then I remember him helping me up from the floor. Five feet away, a regrounded Miss Dyke gracelessly stroked original oak planking as the blood oozed from her nose and split lip. Bar stools were scattered everywhere. The place was dead quiet except for "If" by Bread playing on the sound system.

The bartender, a tough-looking broad in her own right, was just staring down at Miss Dyke and shaking her head softly. She turned to Alan and me and with the voice of experience calmly said, "Just go." We went.

Commercial Street becomes a dark country road not far past the Provincetown business district. It winds through the low dunes, past the nude beach, and out toward the small municipal airport near the start of the high dunes. We were heading out of town at a strange pace, not just slower than Alan ever drove but minus all the usual Alanisms: the way he sat, the way he power-shifted gears, that glancing thing he did on his chin. All in dead silence.

We turned into the airport entrance, stopped at the far end of the empty parking lot facing the runway, and just sat there. A small plane landed, and Alan finally began to talk. His words flowed like he was in some kind of trance.

He remembered flying into this same airport in a Piper Comanche with his mother and father when he was ten. Dad was piloting and he was in the co-pilot seat. At one point Dad told him to take the second wheel. Alan moved it a little too quickly and the right wing dipped, but Dad didn't yell, so Mom had no excuse to overreact. He corrected the dip with Dad's help on the wheel and rudder pedals.

Then the wheel began to feel more comfortable in his hands. Within minutes he and his father were coordinating banks to the right and to the left. They even coordinated the descent. His mother was so proud.

As the plane touched down, Dad let him reduce the throttle, and they taxied to the hangar. Alan said it had been the most wonderful hour of his life.

By the middle of that week his parents were bickering again. By the end of that week, they'd decided to divorce. His mother drove the rented car back to New York City. He and his father rented another one and drove silently to Boston. The Piper Comanche stayed grounded at the airport.

There was a long, uncomfortable silence. Alan took out a business card with the address of the Boston apartment. He sighed deeply: "I have to be alone now." He handed me the card with one hundred dollars and a set of keys.

No. Loody would not be bought off like some whore; like she should just be a nice little bitch and disappear, OK, Honey? *No!* I slapped the card, the cash, and the keys out of his hand.

"Listen to me! I'm taking you to the bus station." "The *fuck* you are!" Suddenly we were screaming at each other. Alan was actually screaming at me. And then I was hitting him, the same man who had saved me from Miss Dyke not an hour earlier.

He stopped screaming, restarted the TR4, and left what little rubber it could in first as Loody kept screaming and pounding him with all her might as she grabbed for the steering wheel, the shifter, the dashboard switches—anything.

After a few deformed, skidding loops around the parking lot, Alan fishtailed us onto the road back to town. The TR4 engine was racing in too low a contested gear and we were swerving all over as he miscrunched his way up to fourth. I got an especially good grip on his hair and the steering wheel. "Get the fuck *offa* me!" He won the wheel back with a hard tug. The TR4 pulled left and all the way across the divider stripe. Somehow he got it (and me) back under control just before we plowed into the dunes.

Alan must have thought I was going to leave it at that. Inconceivably, he'd forgotten [rule one] a shitfaced Loody is incapable of leaving anything. A few deceptively serene seconds later, I lurched for the wheel and this time yanked it completely out of his hands. The TR4 skidded hard right and off the road.

I can recall this numb pain as I landed a perfect slow-motion header into the windshield while I watched Alan smash his face into the steering wheel. I think I may have blacked out.

When my sense of time and place reintegrated, I realized we were in a dead-silent car with no lights on a trafficless road. The nose of the TR4 was pitched up about thirty degrees. The break in the low dunes leading to the nude beach was about fifty feet away. The soft rhythm of low-tide waves was barely audible. Alan's eyes were closed, but from the way his head was shaking back and forth, it seemed entirely by choice.

I shoved my jammed door open, began contorting my way out, and made contact with what I thought was a log. When I finally rested my full weight on it, it compressed in this weird, viscous way.

I knew it [instantly]. I'd killed Jennifer again.

Just beyond the front bumper, a female head lay nearly buried in low dune sand. A deformed bicycle wheel was wedged against the bridge of its nose. Just above the wheel's flattened tire, moonlight reflected off calmly surprised eyes. Just below, bulging mounds of sandy lip and cheek poked through silver spokes. I remember, the alignment of the head and the leg made no sense.

My heart was racing. No. No more Silver Lady nightmares. *No fucking way!*

Alan's eyes opened. I made laser contact with them through the windshield I'd spidered. For the first time I realized there was blood oozing from multiple regions of his face. His head was still shaking softly. I began nodding mine at a much more vigorous pace.

Then [I still don't know how] the trunk of the TR4 lifted open on its own. I darted around, yanked out my backpack, and instantly focused on the illuminated stones of the Pilgrim's Tower, the highest point in Provincetown, maybe two miles away.

"Loody …" The driver's window was opened. By now blood from the deep gash across his nose and upper lip was streaming off his chin. Alan held out the card, the money, and the keys again. His eyes were resigned. As I took it all, he suddenly clutched my hand.

Then he released me.

Roni Pod triple-timed for deliverance as the plan came together with dazzling speed. My destination would be the first bar I could find nearest the one I'd escaped from.

I power-walked in, plopped myself on a barstool, and sat silently. A few lip-quivering seconds later I stifle-sobbed once, cast my eyes skyward, sighed deeply, slowly regained my composure, and ordered my first vodka tonic. Alan would've loved it. I ditched his card and keys in the lady's room and caught the last bus back to New York City.

There was a newsstand on Broadway near the Columbia campus that carried out-of-town papers. Two days later *The Boston Globe* carried a small story about a vehicular homicide in Provincetown. The driver was found drunk in his car with the victim still pinned underneath. He'd refused an attorney, been arraigned, pleaded guilty, was denied bail, and would be transferred to Boston later that week where he'd be remanded until trial.

Neither Alan nor Loody ever returned to Columbia. That first week back, some naïve soul asked if I knew what had happened to him. A fully reconstructed Roni Pod held flat eye contact for three seconds and calmly walked off.

Alan and whoever's head it was now joined my mother and father on the list of people officially barred from my consciousness but who could invade at will. I never [ever] bought another issue of *The Boston Globe* and tried to believe I'd never hear from him again.

One afternoon about two years later I was eating lunch in the Uris Hall cafeteria. I looked up and found my mother standing over me. It was the first time I'd seen her in nearly six years, and it took a few seconds for the image to register.

"Hello, Roni." I instantly resuscitated my unattended antipathy and in a perfectly neutral tone: "What do you want?" Her smile faltered. "I'd like to talk about our family. Is there somewhere we can …"

"I'm late for class." I stood up and strode off. Suddenly, I needed Alan. Desperately. At a minimum I needed to know what had happened to him.

What I didn't know was that Mom had just come from her own mother's funeral. I'd never met my grandmother, knew virtually nothing about her, and simply envisioned her as some variation on Mom. What I also didn't know was my mother hadn't been in contact with either her mother or father in more than twenty-three years, since the day she left for Chicago with me in the oven. At the wake she'd had a long talk with my equally unknown grandfather and learned important things about her parents and herself; the type of things, she sensed, that had the potential to heal. Mom wanted to pass them on to me. She was summarily denied that opportunity and would be similarly denied on several more occasions over the next thirty-plus years.

That weekend I took a flight to Provincetown. I was doing a part-time, paid internship for a [recently ordained] partner at Touche Ross and had more than enough spending money.

The high season had just ended and there were plenty of seats at the Crown & Anchor. Roni Pod manufactured the perfect rationale for her presence and casually lofted inquiries about events from two years earlier with stunning misdirection.

Alan was dead. Murdered. As he was being transferred from the local Provincetown holding facility, Miss Dyke rushed up and stabbed him in the heart. He died instantly. The woman under the TR4 was her live-in lover, the one she cheated on constantly. Her lover responded in kind, not infrequently meeting up with like-minded partners at P-town's all-purpose nude beach. She'd just finished waiting the prescribed time for her most recent paramour to bike it back to town when she met with her untimely end. I reacted credibly.

I flew back that evening committed to staying awake the entire night if necessary to avoid my next long overdue Silver Lady nightmare. Sleep eventually won out, and I dreamt of my mother and father.

They're both about my age and sitting on the blue couch in our upstairs apartment in Uncle Peter's house. Raul is dressed in flowing red robes like some kind of enlightened being. His facial scars have been replaced by an elaborate, colorful tattoo, and there's this soft glow that surrounds him and partially surrounds my mother. I can't hear what they're saying, but the conversation is very pleasant and I'm increasingly upset I'm not part of it.

Finally I shout out, "You will call me *Roni*!" My father turns away from my mother, smiles at me, and in perfect Spanish says, "*Hola* (Hello), Roni." His trill on the R is very pronounced.

Suddenly I'm eight and just standing there like the eight-year-old I should be. I don't know how to respond. He repeats even more kindly, "*Hola*, Roni."

I woke up and forced myself to stay awake for at least another hour. When I calculated it might be safe, I popped a couple of Quaaludes and fell back into the last dreamless sleep of my life.

[My sleep, however induced, would be violently interrupted by any one of several increasingly nightmarish variations on that same dream, every night, for at least the next two years.]

[Countless comparable dreams have followed.]

[You'd never abandon her, not even that fucked-up child, would you, Daddy?]

[Please, Daddy?]

— *Mirona Guzman*

[Oh, Daddy, I love you so much.]

23

RAUL'S 10,272ND LETTER

(RL10272-06281992)

Dear Mirona,

There are things I have shared with you that have upset you, and especially certain details of my life on the streets of San Juan and the West Side. But, sweetheart, we agreed the entire story needs to be told and, even now, there is still a great deal to tell.

By September of 1957, when your mother and grandparents first arrived on West 64th Street, I was already shooting up twice a day and sometimes more. The "more" happened when the heroin I purchased was cut with talc or some other cheap substance and my high came and went in what seemed like no time at all. By that winter, "more" had become the norm.

The money to support my habit came from the usual junkie sources: petty thefts and burglaries, most of them perpetrated against the innocent residents and businesses of the surrounding blocks. Benito would dictate targets and assign roles for the four of us. Our crimes typically relied on stealth and were designed to preserve our anonymity.

Occasionally, however, Benito would engage in a confrontational robbery on his own and would take great pleasure in describing the unnecessary injury he had inflicted. I was initially repulsed by his tactics, then, gradually, just against them for personal security purposes and, finally, didn't care one way or the other so long as there was junk to shoot.

We identified ourselves as members of the Latin Devils. In truth, the Devils existed more in the minds of the police than as a functional organization. To say you were a "Diablo" in those days meant, first and foremost, that you were to be respected in your neighborhood. It also said you would not tolerate the constant harassment of the local White gangs and were prepared to take aggressive action against them.

Word would spread when a confrontation between gangs was in the offing, and any number of subgroups like our own might voluntarily opt in. I did not relish physical violence and usually avoided these frequent events.

However, one night that September, I found myself staggering through Central Park with Benito, Carlos, and Paco. Benito was the only one who knew we were about to meet up with other Devils subgroups to do battle with a White gang called the Jades. The fight was supposed to take place near the northwest end of the boat lake. We were going to ambush the Jades on a narrow footpath.

The different Devils subgroups were meeting up at Bethesda Fountain. I remember being surprised at encountering so many people I knew as we headed for the fountain overpass and may have figured out what was about to happen, but was far too high to care.

The Devils made a noisy descent down the two stairways leading from the overpass to the fountain. I was having a hard time negotiating the steps and fell about halfway. Benito laughed, called me a "maricon," and then just left me sitting there, too stoned to participate or even move.

Just as the last of the Devils reached the bottom of the steps I heard what sounded like a football stadium erupting after a goal. It was the sound of the Jades who were hiding in the dark corridor beneath the overpass. The echo made them sound like some multiple of the forty members the newspaper accounts said they brought with them. The Devils were no more than twenty-five, although the papers put our number at sixty.

I had the perfect seat to the perfect ambush. It all seemed surreal—the running, the screaming, the splashing through the fountain with the chains, then the knives and the guns. Not long after the first shots were fired, I heard the sound of distant sirens.

Then Whites and Latinos were racing and limping up the steps right past me. It was obvious, even to someone in my state, that the Devils had gotten the worst of the encounter by far.

And then there was silence except for those distant sirens. I finally focused on the area just in front of the fountain and made out two motionless bodies lying almost side by side. I managed to stand and stumbled toward them.

One White and one Latino were bleeding from head wounds and were obviously dead. Suddenly Benito was standing next to me with a smoking gun in his hand. He aimed it at the White boy's head just as the sirens began to sound dangerously close. He reluctantly pocketed the gun, spit on the boy, and announced, "Next time I do your mother." Then he laughed, grabbed me by the arm, and dragged me onto some obscure footpath. At some point during our escape he informed me I owed him my life. I had no basis to argue.

The newspaper story identified the Devils as the aggressors. The dead White boy merited a high school yearbook picture; the dead Latino a file mug shot.

Mirona, I'm not trying to identify myself as a victim. You know as well as I do that term is misleading and meaningless. I was simply the result of the energetic forces that were governing my soul at the time, although I was in no condition to recognize those forces or honor their effect.

Nor am I suggesting I was incapable of violence. I most certainly was.

I have to stop now. We will continue this story tomorrow.

And, please, try not to be upset.

I love you, sweetheart.

Daddy

24

RAUL'S 10,273RD LETTER

(RL10273-06291992)

Dear Mirona,

Lydia will be coming to visit this afternoon. Since she quit her housekeeping job and reduced her waitressing to five shifts a week, she has more time to herself and now visits me at least once a month.

As you and I agreed, Lydia knows nothing about our letters. Nor would I ever reveal the intimate details of my conversations with her. What I can tell you is her presence is still a great comfort to me and no small inspiration. Her Energy and her love are as powerful now as they were when I first knew her as a child.

I want to finish the story I began yesterday, before Lydia arrives.

After what happened at Bethesda Fountain, Benito led me through a series of back paths in the park. For a time we could see the flashing lights of patrol cars on the overpass, but trees gradually blocked our view.

Eventually we exited Central Park at West 81st Street, across the street from the Museum of Natural History and the Hayden Planetarium. Benito must have gone off in a different direction the moment we got there. I found myself standing alone in front of one of the wooden benches that line the granite wall surrounding the park. It was very late and I was beginning to come down from my high.

I sat down on a bench and must have passed out. When I came to, the first light of the sun was touching the top of the museum. It looked beautiful on the white granite. A moment later, that beauty was meaningless. I was going into full withdrawal. This was accompanied by a vivid recollection of the two bodies at the fountain, Benito's casual cruelty, and the fact that, somehow, I now owed my life to a violent sociopath. I had no money, no drugs on me or at home, and no idea where my next high was coming from. That high was really all that mattered.

Our apartment was nearly a one-mile walk from where I was and, for the reasons mentioned, going home would do me no good. My mother's welfare check wasn't coming in until later that week, and she would be flat broke by now. When she had cash, she'd learned to leave most of it with a neighbor next door whose son did not place his next high above all else, including family.

It was only a matter of luck that I had not been stopped and questioned by a passing patrol car. I later learned the police had been making regular sweeps of Diablo neighborhoods all through that night and into the morning. Apparently, the upper-class neighborhood surrounding the museum did not merit their attention.

A "C" train passed in the tunnel directly below me. Its rumble and the sweet smell of heated insulation came right up through the metal grating a few feet away. Then I despaired. For the first time in my life I seriously contemplated suicide. My means would be the next C train. I would jump the turnstile, head for the platform, and wait. Or perhaps I would simply jump down to the tracks and step on the 650-volt third rail.

These images were interrupted by those of several alleyways on West 42nd Street in the heart of 1957 Times Square. The images were no less desperate and only slightly less suicidal. They included junkies lying at the back of those alleyways, passed out, comatose, or dead. Some might still have needles sticking in their veins, and some of those needles might contain unutilized heroin.

Times Square was nearly two miles from the museum. The exertion of the walk burned off whatever remaining high I had, and by the time I was snooping through the alleyways, my pain and desperation had reached intolerable levels. One comatose Latino junkie was still holding his works in his hand. There were a few drops of heroin left. The tip of the needle was resting in dirt and rubble that smelled of urine. His tourniquet was still on his arm and his fingers had turned a bluish-red.

I snapped off his tourniquet, put it on my own arm, licked the tip of the needle, and poked for an open vein. The high that followed was minimal.

A few alleyways later I found a young White boy passed out on the ground. His back was against a brick wall and his needle was still stuck in his arm. It had slightly more heroin in it than the last one I had found. As I pulled it out, he came to and kicked at me, and I reflexively planted my heel in his chest. The force of my kick cracked his head against the wall and he was out cold again. Then I repeated what I had done a few moments earlier with slightly more favorable results and no concern for the young man I had just assaulted.

The question now was whether I could last until about 10 a.m. That was when I could score a full hit from a local pusher who showed up briefly in front of a candy store in my neighborhood, even on Sunday mornings. Diablos were sometimes granted credit.

I walked the one mile back very slowly, resting frequently and trying to preserve as much of my weak high as I could. By the time I reached 64th Street, it must have been close to 10 a.m., and the pain and desperation were returning. My path led me directly across the street from Lydia's building.

Mirona, I can never remember a time when I did not feel Lydia was either somehow with me or looking out for me. By the time I was eight, she must have saved my life at least three or four times besides the night when my father and her father and mother were all murdered. Even after she came to New York City she continued to send money to my mother. If she hadn't had the courage to make contact with her half-sister, my mother and I would have never been able to come to 64th Street. Lydia had known the worst life had to offer, and rather than be embittered by it, she felt compassion for those in similar circumstances.

Even at the worst of my addiction, I knew I could always go to her. I never stole a cent from Lydia, not because I wouldn't have, but because she would always offer me the money I needed before I said a word or made a move. She is as close to sainthood as any human I have ever encountered.

That morning I simply could not face her. In fact, I was aware she was looking at me from her window as I plodded by across the street on my quest for that Sunday morning pusher. I also owed her a substantial sum of money that we both knew I would never repay, and I was ashamed.

What I did not know was that I was passing beneath your mother's bedroom window at that very moment. She and her parents had moved into the building across from Lydia's about a week earlier, and your mother's window was directly opposite Lydia's living room window. She and Lydia were staring at each other, recognizing each other in some energetic way. Lydia had not seen your mother in more than ten years, since

Lydia's grammar school graduation. At the time she had recognized a very distinctive Energy pattern in Teresa, and it was manifesting once again.

Beyond that, Lydia saw my Energy pattern rise up and intertwine with your mother's in a way that confirmed our joint paths. Imagine, all this was happening as I was desperately seeking my next hit.

I also did not know your mother had seen me from her window. It was the first time she had seen me since San Juan, and she came running up the block after me. Mirona, she was so overjoyed and so unwilling to recognize what I had become.

Lydia told me about her energetic vision a few weeks later and again the first time I allowed her to visit me here, the week before your mother's visit. She was trying to make me understand my life had a purpose and a future, that it involved your mother, and that she knew all this from an unimpeachable source. I was in no position to appreciate what she was telling me.

She also told me I must someday share this story with someone I love. That was the only time she ever insisted I repeat something she told me here. And so I am.

Mirona, if Lydia had not told me that story, the events following your mother's visit here might have been very different. Although I did not realize it at the time, she had planted a kernel of hope in my soul that would germinate at the very moment when my life hung in the balance just a few days later as I knelt with a cord connecting my neck to the bars of my cell, nearly thirty years ago. What an incredible blessing she is.

I will write to you again tomorrow.

I love you, sweetheart.

Kisses,

Daddy

25

Editor's Commentary On Raul's 10,272nd and 10,273rd Letters

(RL10272(3)C-0628(9)1992-MG1)

I've been married and divorced three times. The marriages all started and ended within a six-year period between my twenty-ninth and thirty-fifth birthdays. Blake was the product of my third and shortest attempt.

I've had countless male encounters but never what most women would identify as a boyfriend. I've also never been "in love" or at least never experienced the sustained, elevated emotions most people and all novelists would describe as love.

Alan was as close as I've ever gotten to either a boyfriend or love, but we never screwed. Gina tells me my hypersexuality was a cry for the romantic love I had no practical way of conceptualizing because of the intense fear frequencies dominating my Soul. As always, what she says makes perfect sense, but to be honest, I've yet to make peace with or "honor" such a glaring deficiency in my life.

Gina says romantic love is still possible for me, but it's wholly contingent on my sustained commitment to suppressing my greatest fears. She also claims I genuinely love my daughter, my mother, my Aunt Lydia, my father, and her. There's one place in this manuscript where I tell my father I love him, and I meant it when I wrote it. But I was also saying it to a man who, while more spiritually vibrant than anyone I've ever known, is still quite dead.

As far as the others, I know I still worry like hell about Blake. She seems more stable now than I've ever known her to be, but I can't help remembering all the grief I put her through, especially after her weekends with her father. And it seems hard to imagine all that can just energetically evaporate.

I wish to God there was some way for my mother to explode and have it out with me for all the grief I've put her through. But she's not me, and that'll never happen. And, again, I get what Gina's saying. I've even experienced the "lightness" [briefly], especially when we were first working together. But the deeper I've gotten into writing this book, the harder it's been not to reconstruct those negative frequencies. I absolutely get what she's telling me. But there they are just the same.

God bless Aunt Lydia. One afternoon, a few weeks ago—I have no idea why—I tried to explain some of my feelings to her. She signaled me to move in closer. When I was in range, she threw this right jab into my left shoulder that I can still feel. Then she hugged me like she wanted to squeeze the life out of me. We downed a few Corona Lights, exchanged a few dirty jokes, and laughed our asses off. Yeah, I do love that woman.

There was this bar in the middle of Clarke Quay in Singapore I used to frequent during business trips. One evening I met the Norwegian captain of some Liberian oil tanker. A few drinks in, we decided it would be fun to try and name all the people we'd ever slept with. He tallied up about fifty women and thought I'd be impressed. My memory gave out at one hundred and thirty-six men. I remember the number. That night made one thirty-seven. I was just twenty-eight at the time.

I've had eight abortions. Two of them involved my first two husbands, both before we were married. The other six were before I received my MBA. Once I began working full-time, I usually took more precautions, if only because abortions demanded a few days away from the job and too many questions.

Marriages one and two were designed to forward some personal agenda items. Not so with number three, David Palmer, Blake's father. If anything, his interests were diametrically opposed to mine.

David was a Harvard MBA. Harvard taught him all businesses could be governed using a single superior formula knowable only to Harvard MBAs. Its strategies placed minimal importance on the nature of the business or its organizational culture and confidently guaranteed corporate perfection through a series of dispassionately developed personnel and operating decisions all dictated from on high by a God who was also a Harvard MBA. It was narcissism masquerading as business science.

Columbia's program took a slightly different approach. It left plenty of room for personal narcissism but, true to its upper west side humanitarian roots, recognized the role of individuals and established cultures in the development of organizational strategies. The Columbia approach was perfect for someone like me. It sanctioned my overtly interpersonal management style and seemed to offer a wink and a nod to the Machiavellian games I reveled in.

David and I met at the least likely of places and events: Martin Luther King Junior Sunday at the Cathedral Church of Saint John the Divine, two blocks from Columbia. [Really.]

About six months earlier I'd returned to what was now Deloitte Touche Tohmatsu after leaving Merrill Lynch, where I'd gone as far as anything with a vagina could go in 1993. The old boys' network there was not only ingrained, it was lapsing into Alzheimer's. I'd already warned them about their research analysts recommending internally managed securities. [Years later it would cost them one hundred million in fines when the New York AG finally caught on to their game. And, for the record, they screwed themselves into that fire sale purchase by BofA with absolutely no help from me.]

Corporate diversity programs were still a rarity anywhere on this planet in 1993, so I was surprised when Deloitte's London office [where I was based] suddenly committed to developing one for worldwide operations. The surprise dissipated when I learned the commitment was linked to a bid for a multimillion-dollar block of NGO business. We lost the bid, but we were still locked into doing that [linked-in] St. John's event.

They needed someone to stand in the pulpit and preach the gospel of diversity. Not surprisingly, the Deloitte board saw mocha-plus, female me as the most likely candidate for the job; the very same candidate who, when she failed to jump for joy at the prospect of self-humiliation, was informed she'd happily volunteered her services. [I'm pretty sure at the time I envisioned myself above both race and gender. Singing the praises of corporate diversity, much less inferring I might be one of its beneficiaries, would have been an utterly repulsive thought.]

With no chance left to turn a profit, it quickly became apparent no one at Deloitte really gave two shits about the Saint John's event, and I was left to my own devices. That meant no need to clear my homily with anyone. And it was a keeper.

David's family had been attending Saint John's since the days when it was a bastion of New York Republicanism as well as the largest cathedral on the planet. He approached me at a reception after the service, complimented me on the great job I knew I'd done, and added whimsically, "You know, at one point I just closed my eyes. And when I opened them … it was still you! Damn, you're good."

It was one of the best backhanded compliments I'd ever received, and it came from this tall, sandy-haired, prep-schoolish creature who looked like he'd just driven in with the top down from Skipster and Muffy's in Amagansett. My entire speech had carefully circumvented any reference to my own skin color. I was playing the role of White girl in blackface, and David had done more than just call me on it. The pompous shit was telling me he was in on it with me. I hated his guts and desperately needed to push off of him. That night at the Sherry-Netherland we had some of the most confrontational sex I can ever remember. Damn, he was good.

At the time I was about five months past my second divorce decree and had gone through, for me, only a small number of the usual consolation types. David was no consolation. He took pleasure in calling me on everything—from the careers I'd destroyed to the words I would imperceptibly slur as I negotiated a level-three buzz, and always with that droll delivery.

Unless and until, of course, he got drunk. Then the WASP filter would clog up and all the crap would back up until it just exploded out of him. If I was relatively sober at the time, I'd toy with him a bit until things got too ugly even for me to deal with.

But if I got drunk with him [and we would do this in unplanned but perfect synch], look out. I was Loody and he was Alan-from-hell returned to give me what I had coming. I explained all this—no, I screamed it at Gina one day, expecting her to compliment me on my insight or at least offer some professional solace.

She laughed and said, "Damn, you're good!" I laughed back for just a second when I realized she was right. Then I walked out on her halfway through the hour with David's exquisite provocations still appended to my list of chronically undrainable frequencies.

We usually had the foresight [read: shared instinct for self-preservation] to get drunk with no one else around. This was because things could get quite physical. Faces were always off limits because, well, they were faces, but pretty much everything else was in play. One morning as we shared a bruised hangover on Riverside Drive [Deloitte had granted my request to relocate to New York], David pithily observed we made Michael Douglas and Kathleen Turner look like sparring partners. I laughed as hard as any number-nine-rib hairline fracture would ever permit. No one at David's venture capital group ever figured out his crutch was taking pressure off a left testicle the size of a ripe pomegranate.

We got married about seven months after our first encounter and were both relatively sound the day of our small civil ceremony. About two months later I got pregnant with Blake during drunken make-up sex [yeah, it could go that way too]. I announced—no, I skewered him with my pregnancy during yet another drunken melee. His not-so-Waspy retort: "That'll teach you a lesson … *Bitch*!"

I called my attorney the next morning and instructed her to draw up the usual divorce papers. This one would be a relatively simple matter, given the brief duration of the union and the strength of the prenup we'd both insisted on. My plan was to head to my gynecologist's office for the usual corrective measures the moment I knew he'd been served. That'd teach him a lesson … *Bastard*!

There are no particular words in my father's two letters that set off my subconscious connections. Of late I've come to recognize what can only be described as planted flavors that stimulate entire sets of memories. Raul's two letters in tandem are Skittles tossed in rice wine vinegar and transport me to the crumb-covered rear seat of a yellow cab driven by a skinny little brown man with a tattered, off-brown turban as we head to 74th Street just off Madison Avenue and my next abortion.

Dr. Rakesh Chandani was a tall, older, elegant Indian and the only nonwhite male to ever get between my thighs. His office was beautiful and his manner amazingly gentle. He was originally recommended to me back at the Columbia clinic by a Black Jamaican nurse who probably thought I'd feel more comfortable being prodded by a man of similar hue.

Rocky, as he let me call him, apologized profusely the first time I saw him as an undergrad for not being able to perform my second abortion in his office. He actually had his nurse accompany me to an East Village clinic to make sure everything came out right. By the time I was teed up for number three, he'd set up all the necessary equipment for in-office procedures. Alan accompanied me to numbers four, five, and six.

All my abortions were preceded by lengthy conversations with Rocky about anything but what I was there for. By seven and eight he knew all about my career and would even bring up errors in some article about me.

He'd usually finish our conversation with something like, "But they've never asked me for a correction … and they had better not!" Then he'd smile. The smile said I was safe here—not wrong, not right, not confused, not vengeful, not homicidal. Just safe. And I was grateful for that. Then he'd do the procedure. He died in 2010. By then I'd been postmenopausal for more than four years and hadn't seen him in at least three. I truly miss that man.

After our pre-number-nine conversation, a particularly long one, Rocky didn't smile. He held gentle eye contact for several seconds and then, with no change of expression: "Roni, isn't there somewhere else you need to be?"

As he said those words, an image of Fred Rogers popped into my brain. It wasn't from one of the serial shows. There was no brilliant Don Costa piano work, no cardigan zipping, no loafer tossing. It was from a PBS special where Fred visited teenagers in a youth detention center somewhere in the Pittsburgh area.

The kids he spoke to were in for everything from drug sales to homicide. It was the last place on earth you'd expect to find Fred.

And he was speaking to these kids as Fred Rogers, the same guy who spoke to me as a nine-year-old, just with an improved vocabulary. He wasn't cool, he wasn't defensive, he wasn't talking down to a bunch of fuckups. He was just validating feelings like he always did.

These kids not only got it, they were literally hanging on every word. One especially tough-looking Latino kid began to tear up. Fred gave a gentle hand signal to his cameraman and the scene cut to black.

I may have been tearing up myself, I'm not sure. When my consciousness returned, I answered Rocky's question: "Yeah." Then—and I'm still not sure why this happened—I stood up, hugged him the way I once hugged Alan at Café Continental [minus the laughter], and just left.

In the cab on the way back to Riverside Drive, I had another out-of-body moment. I'm sitting in the 42nd Street Library staring at the picture of my mother on the cover of the *Daily Mirror*. She's racing down the steps with me in her belly. She's trying to save my life. For all the shame and ostracism she'd already faced and knew she'd still face, she'd be damned if she was going to let them take me from her.

That vision got me through the cab ride and into my building. David had already moved out what little stuff he'd moved in with, and I was fully prepared to spend the prescribed three days of recuperation. Staff had been given all the necessary misdirection, the refrigerator was filled with progressively more tolerable consumables, and the walk-in wine cellar was brimming with the best 20-year-old Pomerol.

As I walked through the front door, I felt that uneasy sensation I've always felt when I knew I was walking into a wrong place. It quickly deteriorated into the hopeless sensation I felt walking home from Jennifer's on Christmas Day. Why? What the fuck had I done wrong this time? How fast could I jumpstart the numbness and maybe add a new layer of skin? I felt even sicker than I normally felt after an abortion.

For some reason I walked to my living room fireplace. In those days there were two framed pictures on the mantle. One was of Rudy Giuliani and me, arms around waists, waving to a crowd from the podium of the New York Hilton ballroom the night of his reelection. [A long story.]

The second was a picture of me on the cover of *Crain's New York Business*. I'm leaning against the front of my desk with me and the best of Manhattan's skyline framed by my office windows. My arms are crossed, I'm holding a royal scepter in my right hand, and my expression is perfected. The caption reads, "The Power Behind The Thrones."

And my thought was, "I'm giving all this up … for what?" I still had my coat on, and I headed for the west terrace. It was early March, and the wind coming off the Hudson was biting. I just stood there staring at the river, at the bare trees below, at New Jersey beyond. I even looked up and behind me to make sure I was still in my penthouse.

And then I allowed myself one sob, just to see how it would feel. Just to prove I could have just one.

I couldn't. The sinkhole finally dropped through me. Instead of a second sob, I heaved my guts up just as I stuck my head out over the railing. The wind blew most of what I retched back in my face and all over my coat.

Then I crumbled. And I cried [for a very long time].

— Mirona Guzman

***

Ed. Note

I sent Gina a copy of this commentary right through that last sentence this morning without first moving it into the "first draft" file. This violated one of her few "technical" writing rules, namely, that every first draft must be deposited in the first draft file to marinate energetically or some such thing. I expected her to get right back to me and insist I move it into the file or gently suggest I give it a more uplifting conclusion. In my cover note, I said I was worried commentaries like this could leave people wondering if the healing power of Energy Medicine wasn't just one big

178

crock. If I could still convincingly reconstruct that same level of pain and find nothing more positive to say about the genesis of my only child, why should anyone take it or me seriously?

I got an email back about 30 minutes ago. After several paragraphs of the usual gushing support, she told me not to change a word and to move this commentary directly to the final draft file. It's the first one to go there. I called and asked her why.

"Listen to your own voice" was all she said. That, and she added there were few people in this world who would ever be loved as much as me.

I'm still crying.

26

Aunt Lydia's Commentaries On Everything—Part 3

(RL1C-05141964-LF3-3)

Mirona: Were you surprised when your father said you had to leave Puerto Rico?

Lydia: No. (shift) Well … they was a lotta things him and me, you know, we don' need to *say* … but I could *see* … they was somethin' on his mind. The … the new Bishop was talkin' to *Spell*-mun, and then he tell my father he don't have to spend so much money on the … the *an*nex. The new school. So … we know somethin' was *com*in'.

Mirona: And you were still living in that caretaker apartment your father built into the annex? All by yourself?

Lydia: (shrugs) Yeah. (pause, elevates) Mirona, was only, like … two blocks from the sheltuh, you know, and Sista Paolo comin' *all* the time … and my father too. I'm just … lookin' after the place, that's all.

Mirona: Were you always there just … by your*self?*

Lydia: Yeah, since I was, I dunno …like … *ten?* (shift) Well, 'cept for one time when I was like … eleven. My mother, one time, she was tryin' to get away from Jesús, you know? So one day, she … she just walk *right* into my apartment.

And that day my *Popi* (Daddy) there with me. And I was *cry*in' 'cause that day … I don't know why, I jus' … I feel like … (softly, taps chest) I'm a little kid, you know? (smiles) First time in my life … I'm *feel*in' like that. So I'm lyin' on the bed and I'm *cry*in', not 'cause I'm *sad* so much but … I'm feelin' like … (smiles) I just wanna *cry.* You know what I'm sayin', Mirona?

Mirona: (pause, softly) Yeah.

Lydia: And my father sittin' next to me on the bed, touchin' my hair … tryin' to make me feel better, you know?

And then my mother just walk in. And she say … I remember … She say, (gruffly) "So *tha's* why you build this … this *kid*die *love* shack? Leas' I was fourteen when you done *me!*" (pause, softly, head shake) Tha's what she say. (pause) Uhm.

(shift) And *jus'* after she say that, Jesús come in. And he lookin' for her 'cause, you know … he *need* her for his, uh … sou-*pli*-uhs.

So he *yell*in' at my mother and actin' like me and my father ain't even *there!* An' my father say to him (points finger), "Get …

out … *now!*" And then Jesús say (mockingly), "Who the hell are you? Who the fuck you think you *talk*in' to?"

Heh! And then my father *stand* up and, you know, all … (gesturing) all dress' up like a Mon*sign*or! And he (strong gestures) *grab* Jesús by the back of the neck, and he jus' … he jus' *throw* him outta the apartment.

And Jesús … Heh! He get all *crazy* and he *yell*in', "*Nobody do this to Jesús! I gotta lotta friends! You gonna have a lotta problems!*" (scoffs) But he don't do nothin'. And he just take my mother back with him.

But my father say to me, (softly) you know … 'cause … he know what I was *think*in' … He say, (slowly) "Lydia, your mother can stay with you, but only when she sober." (pause, gently) I really love that man.

Mirona: (long pause, childlike) Did your mother stay with you?

Lydia: One night. Jus' … one night, maybe … few months later. She knock on the back door, and I let her in. She look like … (resigned) OK, she wasn' *so* high. And I'm thinkin', you know, maybe … So I sleep on the couch and I let her use the bed.

Middle' the night, I hear … she walkin' aroun', you know, *look*in' at stuff. And then I hear the door open … and then it close … real quiet. (pause) An' tha's it.

Mirona: (pause) And … did you …

Lydia: (over her, flatly) No. No, next time I seen her was the night she get kill'. (knocking on door)

Mirona: (to Jason) Were you expecting someone?

Jason: (in distance) Nobody. (pause) It's locked. Should I …? (more knocking)

Mirona: Yeah. Go see. (footsteps, door opens)

Blake: (in distance) Thanks, Jason … (door closes)

Mirona: (annoyed) Beebs, what are you doing here? I told you to take an Uber back to …

Blake: (over her) Mom!

Mirona: (over her) You know, at this hour, this neighborhood isn't exactly …

Blake: (over her, stronger) Ma! Aunt Gina said you guys would still be here, OK? And I just … I just want to *listen*, OK? That's all.

Lydia: Hey, Mirona! Come on! I's nice to have another … *pretty* girl hangin' roun'. (to Blake) Make me feel kinda … (shoulder twitch) *sexy*, you know? (Blake laughs) Go get you'self a *cerveza* … an' get me one, too!

Blake: (sound of footsteps, sarcastically) They *cold* yet?

(*Five minutes later*)

Mirona: So … why'd you go to Jesús's house that night?

Lydia: (shrug) 'Cause I gotta pick up *Raul!*

Mirona: But I thought you said you wouldn't let him go there to …

Lydia: (over her) No … well … (calming gesture, pause) OK, when Raul maybe … five?, one day his mother, Celia, she come to me and she say, (finger waving) "A boy need to see his *father!*"

And I say to her, "What? You *crazy*? You want Raul to be with Jesús? And my *moth*er? You know wha's goin' *on* in that house?"

But Celia wasn' *doin'* so good. She still livin' in the *shel*tuh but now she cleanin' houses *too*, you know? An' she got that big, uh … the, uh … the *scar* on her face.

And she the one everybody use' to say, "Holy shit, she so *beau*-ty-ful!" And they pay more *mon*ey for her. Even she's a whore, you know, 'cause … she was *spec*ial.

But now she thinkin', "I got *noth*in'." She ain't *think*in' right 'cause … she listenin' to Jesús. (elevates) An' Jesús? Heh! He *real*ly got nothin'! But he figure (macho voice), "Hey, I got Raul. And tha's gonna make me feel *bet*ter, ya know, like a *real* man … with a *son*!" Heh!

So Jesús keep talkin' to Celia, and finally she start to be*lieve* him, to … to *think* like him. Tha's when she tell me, she want Raul to go see his father.

Now … Raul still goin' a school. And most of the time, after school, he don't go back to the shelter 'cause Celia … (sighs) OK, you know … sometime she still workin' … after she done her cleanin'. And she don't get home till *real* late. Maybe next day. So … Raul stay with me.

So I tell Celia, "Only way Raul gonna see Jesús is if *I* take him there and then *I* pick him up. Few hours. Tha's it. Maybe … once a week." And Celia, you know … (resigned shrug) She say, "OK."

Now … when Raul start to see Jesús, I'm maybe … fourteen. And for a little while we go almos' every week. But then, Jesús …

Heh! Now he *usin'* more shit then he *sellin'*! And then for a long time he just for*get* about Raul. Maybe almost two years!

(shift, to Blake) You eat yet, baby? They's some pizza. Use the, uh … the *mi*crowave. And they's … *wings* … in the 'frigerator. *Cuidado!* (Be careful!) They *hot*.

Blake: (goofy histrionic) Golly, Aunty Lyd! Cold pizza, warm beer, and hot wings! (humorous Latin accent) *Eet* don' *ged* no *bet*tuh den *dat*! (laughter)

Lydia: C'mere! (comic confusion) I think I'm s'pose to *slap* you … (L/B laugh, chairs move, light slaps).

Mirona: (over them, reprimanding) Guys … guys … look, it's getting … can we just? …

Lydia: (mid-goofing) Hey! Mirona! Relax! We just … you know …

Mirona: (over her, sudden aggression) *Look*! There's just so much *shit*! I'm … (long pause, composes)

Lydia: (knowing smile, conciliatory) Is OK … Is OK. (long pause, shift) So I'm hearin' all *kind*a shit, like Jesús ain't payin' his sou-*pli*-uz on time. And *then* I hear … he ain't payin' them for a few *weeks*! And, you know, you can't *do* that! And then I hear his sou-*pli*-uz ain't even doin' it with my *moth*er no more! Is only the *mo*ney now! And he owe them a *lot*ta money.

Middle all *this* shit (head shake) … Uhm! One day Celia tell me Jesús wanna see *Raul* again! And I tell her, "*No*! You *crazy*? … Is too *dan*gerous there." But … she don't care. He playin' with her *head* again, you know? So … what can I say?

So coupla days later I take Raul to Jesús at his house … abou'
… two o'clock. And I can *see*, Jesús ain't *shav*in'. He smell like …
like *shit*! All fucked up! And then I'm lookin' at his lights, you
know … and they look like the same lights from the guy who try
to kill my mother dat time when I was little. Uhm!

So now I'm standin' at the front door … with Raul. And, all of
a sudden, Jesús just (abrupt gesture) *grab* him, like this. And then
he … (gestures) *slam* the door!

So I go aroun' de back and there's this … this *bust*ed window.
And I see Raul just sittin' on the couch … in the livin' room. All
by himself. And he seen me, and he (gestures) wave his hand,
like this. Like, (sweetly) "Is OK. Don't worry. I'm with my *Popi*."
(wistfully) Little kid. Uhm!

(shift) So I start walkin' home. But then I seen this car drivin',
reeeeal slow! The two sou-*pli*-uz is in the car and they lookin' *right*
at the house. They ain't even *look*in' at me! And they just keep
drivin'. But I know. This ain't gonna be *good*.

So when I get home I start makin' dinner 'cause my father
comin' over. And I told him I gonna make his favorite *arroz con
pollo* (chicken with rice). (secretively) I make it *so* good that night!

So after dinner … we start talkin'. And I know he got somethin'
he wanna say. So he say he find out the new Bishop gonna shut
down the annex … *real* soon … an' he gonna send my father someplace … (gestures) he don't even know *where*. And he ain't gonna be
able to take care of his daughter no more … like a father sup*pose* to.

And then he tell me he got this friend, in New York, 'nother priest from Spain, like him, and he run a shelter on Sixty-four' Street … and I can *live* there. And the other priest can help me get a job and then find a place to live. Like an a*part*ment, you know?

So I feel really *bad,* but … (shrugs) he just doin' what he can *do.* Tryin' to find a way … to *help* me … like he done. (long pause)

Then I look at the clock in the kitchen and is time to go pick up Raul. And I tell my father, "Is OK, I can walk." But he say, "No! Tonight I wanna drive my daughter." (remembers, smiles) He got a car 'cause … he' the Mon*sig*nor, but … we don't want no people to see us like that.

But, you know, now is *dark* outside, so I say, "Thank you, Popi" … and I give him a big hug. (introspective pause) And then we go pick up Raul. (long pause, deep sigh)

Mirona: (with concern) Aunt Lydia, do you wanna …?

Lydia: (assertively) No … *No!* (taps her chest) So I'm in the car with my father. And when we, maybe … two blocks away from Jesús I seen *fire* comin' from a house. And … and I'm not thinkin', you know, is Jes*ús,* but then a coupla seconds … I can *see!* Is his *house!* And I'm tellin' my father, "*Popi! Popi!* Go *fast!*" 'Cause I know *Raul* is in there!

And in fronna the house I seen de pimp. And he … he *laugh*in'! … like a *crazy* man! And he got this *gun* in his hand.

And on the ground in fronna the house I seen Jes*ús!* (visualizing) On *fire!* An' … an' his *clothes* is burnin'. (pause) But … he ain't movin' … (gestures, softly) 'cause … (re-elevates) And they's *flames* comin' outta the *win*dows! And the pimp got a *bot*tle in his hand wit' a … a *rag* in it. And then he light the rag on fire and he throw the uh … the, uhhh …

Blake: (over her, hypnotically) Molotov cocktail …

Lydia: Yeah. He throw it in the *win*dow. I mean, the place is al*ready* burnin', you know? … He was *crazy*!

And then … (softly) then I seen my *mot*her come runnin' outta the front door. She … (diminishes) she musta been *real* high an' … an' I guess … the flames, they … they wake her up an' (sighs) … she musta … (shrugs).

So when she come outside, the pimp *seen* her … and he hold his gun (two-handed pose) like this … and … (taps chest twice, intense whisper) right there (dropping gesture).

(elevates) So then the pimp seen *me*! And he start walkin' to me and he shoutin', "Ugly little *bitch*! You fuck up *my* life? Now I'm gonna fuck *you* up!" And I *know* … you know … he talkin' about when me and Celia get the money from all the *men*! (waves finger) He *nev*er forget that!

(staring pause, shrugs) So now I'm waitin' for him to *kill* me. (intensely) And all of a sudden my *fath*er, he jus' … he run *right* in fronna me! And he *scream*in', "No!" And when he done dat … I don' know why, ah jus' … ah jus' look across the street. And I seen the two su-*pli*-uz sittin' in the same car … jus' … *watch*in'.

(silence, distant stare) An' den … (taps chest twice, staring pause).

And my father, he just (longer staring pause, weak gesture) fall *back*. And I'm tryin' to hold him up, but ... but he too *big* for me, you know? (pause) And ... and then he fall *down* ... with his back ... *right* on top of me. So, like, (gestures, diminishing) his *face* ... right next to *my* face. And he ... coverin' me up ... with his whole body.

And I tell him (soft intensity), "*Popi, Popi! Please*, don't die! *Please!*" (distant stare) An' he just ... *look*in' at me ... tryin' to smile. (long pause) And then he say to me ... (reliving it) "Tell her ... Tell her ..." (very long silence, Blake begins to sob)

Blake: I ... I can't ... (cries like a child) Mommy! Mommy, don't die! ... (Mirona hesitates, then takes Blake's hand.) Please, Mommy! Don't! ...

(Lydia begins to gently stroke Blake's hair and shoulders. Mirona's confused eyes remain locked on Blake.)

(*10 minutes later*)

Lydia: And then the pimp say, "Aw, *fuck!*" And he start *walk*in' to me 'cause he still wanna *kill* me, you know! (to Blake, with gentle humor) Don't worry, baby! He don't kill me! (Blake sniffles a chuckle) He tryin' to walk to where he can *shoot* me 'cause, you know, my father still on *top* of me.

(revelation) And all of a sudden, I ... I seen this *light* ... from my *fath*er! I ain't never *seen* a light like that before! And I *know*, he *tell*in' me, "Lydia! Scream! Scream!" I just *know*. So I start to *scream!* And I'm screamin' (reliving it) "*Ayuda! Ayúdame!* (Help me!) He kill my mother and my father! *Ayúdame!*"

(powerfully) And *just* before the pimp gonna *kill* me? ... I seen from the car (gestures, loudly) *Bam! Bam! Bam! Bam!* ... *Four* shots ... And the *pimp?* ... (slaps table) *Down ... Dead.*

(intense stare) An' right after that, I feel my *father*, his ... his *alma* (soul) ... his, uh ... his ... *espíritu* (spirit) ... pass *right* through me! And I *know* ... my Popi feelin' *good!* (soft chuckle) He know he done a *good* thing for me! (smiles) He still lookin' after his *daugh*ter! (internal pause)

Then I seen de guy, de sou-*pli*-uh, with the *gun* ... in the *car*. (points) And he lookin' *right* into my eyes! And *just* when he done that, the other sou-*pli*-uh hit him *right* in the face ... with his fist and he yellin', "Fuckin' *id*iot! Now we gotta do the *bitch!*"

So the guy with the gun, he start to get outta the car, but de other guy say, "*No!* ... Now we gotta get *out*ta here!" 'Cause ... we startin' to hear the, uh ... the *sirens* ... from *La Hara*.

So the car start to go *real* fast! An' when they go *by?* The guy who shoot the *pimp?* He just *star*in' at me like ... like he gonna ... (intense gesture)

(shift) And then ... I re*member!* ... *Raul!* He still in the *house!* So I ... (gestures) I *push* my Popi offa me and I *run* to the back of the house, to the busted window. And I seen Raul just ... *standin'* in fronna the couch. ... (diminishes) *quiet*, like he's havin' a *dream* or somethin'. The fire ... all aroun' him but ... it still ain't *touch*in' him. So I ... I open de window and I climb in and ... (long pause, weak gesture) I don't know how ... I jus' ... I got him *out*.

(increasingly trancelike) So now they's a lotta people startin' to come aroun' … lookin' at my mother and Jesús … and my father … and the pimp.

Raul jus' … he jus' walk up to Jesús … jus' … lookin' at him. And he don't *say* nothin' … jus' …

And I'm lookin' at my father … then back at my mother. (long pause)

Then he standin' next to me … Raul … jus' … lookin' at me like … *empty.* (pause) An' I'm lookin' at him. And then we start to walk away. (long pause)

After a while, I jus' … you know, I gotta *stop* … and I look … again. And I'm watchin' *La Hara* pick up my father and they … they put him in the back of the car. Like … in a *dream.*

And then … they gone. (long pause) And they leave my mother … and Jesús… and the pimp … on the ground. (pause) *Right* there.

Jus' … (stares off, pause, weak gesture, barely audible) right there.

27

RAUL'S 10,294TH LETTER

(RL10294-07201992)

Dear Mirona,

This morning, I learned that one of the oldest prisoners here has died. He was in for nearly sixty-three years and was eighty-one years old. Only last year, he decided to take my introductory writing class and did very well. We became friends and began to share many things about our pasts. There were times when I found myself talking about things I hadn't thought about for years. I was amazed by the level of detail I could recall when I was speaking with him.

And then, this morning, when I heard he was dead, I suddenly remembered some things I thought I would never remember. But there they were. I hope you will let me tell you about them.

One day, when I was about five years old, my mother came to the caretaker apartment late in the evening. I was supposed to be asleep. I heard her and Lydia arguing about my father. It was the first time I'd ever had confirmation he existed. Lydia and my mother were negotiating the terms under which I would see him, and I was thrilled. It was clear, however, Lydia did not share my enthusiasm.

Not long after that, Lydia took me to my father's house. I remember them arguing at the front door, and the next thing I knew, I was alone in the house with him.

My father's name was Jesús Guzman. He was probably in his early thirties at the time. I remember that first moment alone with him; he just stared into my eyes, then smiled and tousled my hair. Then his expression seemed to change. He told me to sit on the couch in the living room, and I did. I was overjoyed. I had done what my father asked.

Most of my time during that first visit and most of the visits after that was spent sitting on that couch. My father would go off and, occasionally, I would hear him talking to someone in another room. Once, a woman I did not know came into the living room, stared at me for a moment, then turned and left. Years later Lydia told me it was her mother. She was living with my father and was involved in his retail drug business.

Sometimes my father would stagger back into the living room, plop down on the couch next to me, and pass out. I would look at him, sleeping, and then try to position my body just like his. I would even try to take a nap, just like my father was taking.

He told me had been raised in an orphanage and had been living on the streets by himself since he was twelve. He wanted me to know he had accomplished a great deal for someone starting out with so few advantages. And he especially wanted me to know he was respected by other people and deserved my respect as well.

I might have visited him six or seven times after that, always with Lydia dropping me off and picking me up. Then there was a long gap when there were no visits. I remember inventing all sorts of reasons for not seeing him and explaining these reasons to the other children at the annex. He was a very important man who had many important things to do. He did not have a lot of time to see me, but he would. I was positive.

After what became a hiatus of nearly two years, Lydia again took me to see my father. By now I was seven and, even with all the protection Lydia gave me, was rapidly surrendering what little naïveté I had left.

This time I was immediately aware of the foul odor in my father's house. His arms were covered in needle tracks and he had lost a great deal of weight. He just stared at me and then walked out of the room. There were no words or conversation of any kind. I sat down on that same couch. It was filthy and littered with broken hypodermic needles and burnt bottle caps. I picked one up and sniffed it. It had the sweet musty odor of cooked heroin that would become so familiar just a few years later.

Then I forced myself to nap. I must have slept for several hours.

I was awakened by the sound of a man yelling and, immediately after that, glass breaking. It came from the bedroom. Seconds later, there was another crash through the kitchen window. I could see the kitchen from where I was sitting. Flames were spreading quickly. Looking back toward the bedroom, I could see the glow of flames on the wall opposite the doorway.

Then I heard my father start to scream. His screams were horrible. I have never heard sounds like that, before or since.

He came staggering out of the bedroom into the living room. My father was on fire. His pants, his shirt, and his hair were all burning. He was swatting at himself and just screaming. For a time he just spun about in the living room not three feet away, and I thought he was going to fall on me. Then, suddenly, he lurched for the front door, somehow opened it, and stumbled through. Then I heard two gunshots and he stopped screaming.

I'd barely had time to process this when Lydia's mother staggered into the living room. She was making a throaty sound I've never heard another person make. I don't think she was wearing any clothing. Most of her body was covered in what looked like small black and red bubbles. She stopped and faced me for a moment and flapped her arms as if she were trying to fly.

Suddenly, another Molotov cocktail crashed through the front window just opposite where I was sitting and hit Lydia's mother in the back. It bounced off her and rolled toward the wall. Flames began to consume the wooden floor.

Then she staggered out the front door. I heard two more shots. And then I heard a man's voice shout, "No."

There were two more gunshots. Then I heard Lydia start to scream. And there were even more gunshots.

Later I remember walking up to my father lying on the ground. The flames had gone out, but there was still smoke rising from what was left of his clothes and his skin. I could not make out his face.

My only thought was, I should have told him. I should have run into the bedroom and I should have told him I heard the glass break. I could have woken him up. I could have saved my father, and I had failed.

The next thing I remember was walking home with Lydia. We went to her apartment in the annex. I sat on the couch while she made me some food. Finally she said, "Raulito, you've got to sleep. I want you to sleep now." She said it very softly, very kindly, as if it was advice she herself wanted to follow.

I remember waking up on the couch and hearing Lydia talking with Sister Paolo. Sister sounded very worried. As I pretended to be asleep, I saw Sister hand Lydia some money. They hugged and Sister left.

I couldn't fall back asleep. I kept trying to suppress the image of my father on the ground. And my guilt. Finally, when I could suppress it all no longer, I began to cry.

Lydia came rushing into the living room, sat on the couch next to me, and began hugging and rocking me. We both cried for what seemed like forever. The crying made me feel just the slightest bit better. Then I must have fallen asleep.

When I awoke the next morning, my mother and Sister Paolo were in the apartment. We all started walking back to the shelter. My mother was carrying my clothes and would not look at me. Sister Paolo had her arm around my shoulder and would only smile. When I asked her where Lydia was, her smile broadened.

I lived in that shelter until I ran off when I was twelve, just like my father. And I began to live very much the way I imagine he must have lived.

The next time I would see Lydia would be on West 64th Street when I was eighteen years old and doing very much what my father was probably doing when he was eighteen.

Mirona, I apologize for telling you such a sad story. But I needed to tell you. And I'm so thankful to you and proud of you for listening. I knew you could.

I love you, sweetheart.

I will write again tomorrow.

Kisses,

Daddy

28

EDITOR'S COMMENTARY ON
RAUL'S 10,294TH LETTER

(RL10294C-07201992-MG1)

There've been days when I've read this letter ten times. And each time I try to start writing a commentary, I freeze. So I read the letter again with no time or space in between. And it's the same. Every time. I can't start it and I can't finish starting it.

My mother and Blake and Aunt Lydia and Gina have all started and finished whatever they needed to start and finish. Not me. I'm like the Steely Dan song: *"You go back, Jack, do it again, wheels turnin' 'round and 'round."*

I used to love that song.

Until I figured out what the fuck it really meant.

— Mirona Guzman

29

Aunt Lydia's Commentaries On Everything—Part 4

(RL1C-05141964-LF3-4)

Mirona: So you never finished the story the other night.

Lydia: Mirona, all I'm *doin'* is tellin' stories! What story you talkin' about?

Mirona: What happened that night … after your father … and how you got to New York.

Lydia: (quizzically) I didn' *tell* you about that? You *sure*?

Mirona: You were …

Lydia: (sipping coffee, over her) Ugh! They's no *sug*ar!

Mirona: (frustrated) I put *three* sugars! …

Lydia: (over her) I tol' you … *five*!

Mirona: How can? … Are you sure you're not diabetic?

Lydia: I ain't *noth*in'! (laughs)

Mirona: Yeah? You keep that up and …

Lydia: (over her) Hey! Mirona! Just get me two sugars, OK? (chair moving, footsteps, pouring/mixing sounds, loud sip) Ah! … Yeah.

Mirona: (sarcastically) I'm *so* glad. (Lydia chuckles) Sooo … that night. Now you're home and …

Lydia: Yeah … so … coupla hours later Sista Paolo come to the apartment. She got de, uh, key, so she just come in. And she already *know* what happen. Heh! The whole fuckin' *bar*rio know! And she say to me, "These guys, they still wanna *kill* you! You gotta get *out*ta here!" And then I tell her about the shelter in New York.

And then she say, "You gotta *go*! *Now*! Tomorrow mornin' you gotta fly to New York." And then she give me some money … for the ticket.

And then I give her a big hug and a kiss 'cause … (sadly) I know. I ain't gonna see her no more.

So I got this old straw bag and I start to put my *stuff* in it. And then I tie the, uh … the *string* around it. Then I go sit in the kitchen and I'm waitin' for the first *guagua* (bus) to de airport. About … five thirty.

So just before I'm gonna leave, somebody knock on the door. And I get *real* scare' 'cause, you know, maybe is the sou-*pli*-uz!

But then … I could *feel* … is not them. So … so I open the

door and is Celia. And … she wearin' wunna her dresses from when she was workin'. And she just *look*a me like … *empty*. Uhm!

So I give her the key to the … to the *school* … and the apartment. Same key. And I tell her, "Raul's OK, don' worry. He's asleep. I'm gonna help you and him after I go to New York." (pause, compassionately) And then she just start to *cry*. Real quiet. And … and she lookin' at her dress, you know? And then she lookin' at me, and … (gestures) she cover her face, like this.

Mirona: (questioning pause) You had no *tick*et! … no reserva-tion. How could you even …?

Lydia: (over her, chuckling) Mirona! I don't know *shit* about this stuff, OK! I never even been outta San *Juan*. And now I'm gonna fly on a *plane*? *Me*? Heh!

But … you know … I gotta *go*! So now I'm on the *guagua*, lookin' around, thinkin', you know, maybe somebody work for the sou-*pli*-uz! The whole time, I'm just … lookin' at the *lights* … tryin' to make sure, you know?

So I get to the airport and I go to the, uh … uh … the *count*er … where you buy the ticket. And I say to the lady, "I wanna go to New *York*." An' … an' she *look* at me like, (scoffs) *Yeah, sure!* Then she say (snooty), "That will be one hundred and eighty-six dollars … *please*."

And then, I remember. I never count how much Sister *give* me! (resigned shrug) But … I figure, you know, no way I got *that* much. So I just give the lady everything I got. And she start to count.

And when she done … she start *writin'*! And then she give me a *tick*et … and *four do*llars! Sister give me *one hund*red and *ninet*y *do*llars! And I know, that was, like … *ev'*rythin' she *got*! (thoughtful pause, soft intensity) She was *so* good to me.

So I fly to New York. And I'm lookin' down from the plane and I can't believe how *big* it is and all the *build*ings!

And finally I get to Sixty-four' Street … and I find the shelter. And I meet Father Zarlino. He … (gestures, chuckles) he's a *litt*le guy, almost like me, and he's wearin' these, uh, the *brown…* things. For Saint Francis, you know?

Mirona: He was a Franciscan priest.

Lydia: Yeah. So I say, "I'm Lydia." And right away … he know who I am. He tell me my *Popi* call him 'bout two weeks ago.

And then he ask me, "How's he *do*in'?" (long pause, sad chuckle)

And we sit down … and I tell him what happen … (very softly) An' then he put his hands over his mouth … (gesture) like this … and then he start to cry … And all the time he just lookin' … *right* into my eyes, you know?

So then I tell him, just before my Popi die, he tell me …, (intensely) "Tell her. Tell her." And Padre Zarlino … he just *look* at me! And his eyes get *big* … and then he start to *smile*! Tha's when he tell me … I gotta *sister* … my *half*-sister. Her name was (slowly) Alina *Weed*-wort.

Mirona: (surprised) What's the last name?

Lydia: (struggling) *Weed* … wort …

Mirona: Whitworth! Right?

Lydia: *Yeah*, tha's what I *said*!

Mirona: (elevating) Alina Whitworth? One-twenty-eight Central Park South? Twelfth floor? She died … six years ago, in her nineties, with about a hundred and fifty million and left most of it to charity? We're talking about the same Alina Whitworth?

Lydia: *Yeah*! A*li*na!

Mirona: (pause, incredulous) She was your half si …? How!? … (stops herself) Yeah … I know *how*, but … (pause, shift) OK, just … tell me the story.

Lydia: (smiles) How come you know Alina?

Mirona: She was one of my private wealth clients at Morgan Stanley. The last few years before she died she began supporting a whole range of charities and …

Lydia: (over her) Yeah! Alina done a *lot*ta good stuff!

(shift) OK, so … Padre Zarlino tell me I got a half-sister, Alina. My Popi and her mother grow up in Spain together. Her family want her to marry this, uh … this *Eng*lish guy … *Weed*-wort … and my *Popi*'s family want him to be a *priest*! But they really *love* each other, you know? So … what happen? (shrug) Heh! She marry Weed-wort and my Popi become a priest! (laughs)

So they send him to Puerto Rico. And right away, they make him the Mon*sig*nor 'cause … his *fam*ily … you know. (elevates) But he was a *good* Monsignor!

So … Alina's mother come with *Weed*-wort, here, to New York. (remembering) I think her name was, uh … Cecilia.

Mirona: Yeah! Burt and Cissy! The king and queen of New York society … until Pearl Harbor. And then the murder-suicide.

Lydia: Yeah, well … the *queen* wasn't so happy with the *king*, you know? Always messin' around … and tryin' to keep it *real* quiet. But even when she's a little kid, (shakes finger) Alina know wha's goin' on.

So my father write to her mother and he tell her, "Cecilia, I'm comin' to New York for a meeting. And I *miss* you and I still *love* you." Cecilia feel the same way … and she go to see him … And she get … *embarazada*! (shrug) And tha's Alina.

Mirona: (slack-jawed, softly) Holy …!

Lydia: (shift) Now … Padre Zarlino tell me I gotta go *see* Alina and tell her who she *is* … what happen to her *real* father … and I'm her *sister*. That's what my Popi want me to do. So I go to her building.

Mirona: On Central Park South! Yeah, I've *been* there!

Lydia: Yeah. And I seen Alina walkin' in. The padre tell me what she look like, so … so I *know*. (intensely) She was *beau-ty-ful*! All … *brown* hair, all … *up* and she's wearin' a beau-ty-ful dress, you know, in the *summer*. An' she walkin' like a … like a *queen*!

She musta been … (looks off) if I'm sixteen, she musta been … twenny-seven.

So I tell the doorman, I gotta *see* her. But I don' say it like that. The padre tell me to say, "Please tell Miss Weed-wort another girl with green eyes need to talk to her." And the guy just *look* at me, you know? (chuckles)

So I go across the street and I'm sittin' on the bench, just lookin' at *him*! And he still *look*in' at me. All day. And now is startin' to get *dark*!

So then I seen him pick up the telly-phone and he talkin' to somebody. An' … an' then he move his hand to me (gestures "Come here"), like this.

And then he put me in the *el*evator … *beau*ty-ful! … with the guy who run it. And he take me up to, uh …

Mirona: (over her) … Yeah! On the twelfth floor!

Lydia: Yeah. So I ring the bell, and Alina open the door. You know, she got the same green eyes, like *me*. And we both lookin' and we not *say*in' nothin'. So then I say, "Our father want you to know about him." Father Zarlino tell me to say that, too. And, you know, she's still *look*in' at me. But then she say, "Please come in."

And I tell her the story. And she still not *say*in' nothin'. Just lookin' into my eyes. And now I'm lookin' at the lights comin' from *her*.

And then … (with confusion) all of a sudden, the lights go a*way*! And I got *scared*! And I say to her, "Can you see the lights?" So she turn around and she look through the windows 'cause, you know, is dark and you can see all the lights in the park from there. And then she talk to me like she think I'm bein' like, you know … like a *smart* ass. And she say, (with an edge) "What lights?"

And I just get up … and I walk to the door. And then all of a sudden she say, "*Wait* a minute, *wait* a minute! Didn' you come here for somethin' *else*?"

I know what she tryin' to say, you know? But … I just look at her and I say, "No, nothin' else. Goodbye, Alina." And then I go.

Heh! Abou' nine years later, I get this letter from Alina … with a *note*. And all it say is … "I can't explain it." And then she sign her name: "Alina, *Weed*-wort … *Fuen*tes." (smiles, softly) Hmm! And inside the note they's *ten fifty-dollar bills*! *Five hundred dollars*! (chuckles, shrugs) So tha's the money I use to bring Raul and Celia to New York.

(shift) But I'm still not seein' no lights. Almost … ten *years*. And the first time I seen them again was the day I seen Raul walkin' under you' mother's window. (smiles) The lights from *him*, they go up and they … they come together with the lights from Teresa. I told you 'bout that, right?

Mirona: (long pause) Can I ask you something?

Lydia: What?

Mirona: After Alina died, when we were executing her estate, there was this document that said a small portion had already been distributed as a personal bequest. There was no beneficiary and no other information. Do you know anything about that?

Lydia: (matter-of-factly) You talkin' 'bout the money she give *me*?

Mirona: It … that was *you*?

Lydia: (casually) *Yeah*! She give me like … I think was about … five … no … *six* million dollars.

Mirona: (flabbergasted) What?

Lydia: *Yeah*! I give one million back to, uh … to the, uhhh … the *law*yer who was givin' the money to all the other … *cha*-ri-ties Alina was givin' to.

Mirona: (numb, softly) Elliott Beckstein … He never …

Lydia: (over her) Yeah, *Elly*-ott! Nice guy. And I wanna give some money to the *shel*ter but … is not there no more, you know? And Sister die a *long* time ago. The … the *gov*ernment … in San Juan, they … well, they *try*in' to do some stuff like that now.

Oh! And I give a *lot*ta money to help dem make a new, uh … *school*! … for 'bout two hundred little kids. Is open now … almos' *two* years! (proudly) "The Monsignor Fuentes School." You know, for my father.

(shift) And I keep a little money here, and the guy at the bank … *nice* guy … he let me know how much I got.

(Mirona stares blankly at Lydia and begins tearing up.) What's the matter, baby? … What's the matter? (chair moves, footsteps, Lydia strokes Mirona's head and shoulders)

Mirona: Why can't? … What is it you? … Why do I … *nev*er!? … (Mirona weeps uncontrollably.)

Lydia: (very kindly, softly) Is OK. I know … I know. Is OK, sweetheart.

30

RAUL'S 19,087TH LETTER

(RL19087-08162016)

Dear Mirona,

I have very good news. The warden approved my request to participate in the experimental drug program. Late last night I was moved by ambulance to Phelps Memorial Hospital, a few miles south of the prison.

We were both expecting his approval. Still, I am the only prisoner in the program, and my current age and condition place me just barely within the limits of its target demographic. But here I am, just the same.

I made the trip in an ambulance even though I felt well enough to take the prison bus. The transportation protocols required me to travel strapped to a gurney. I was facing the two windows in the rear doors of the ambulance, so my view was angled upwards the entire way.

And what an amazing trip. We passed through gates and fences I had last passed through as a teenager sitting on the prison bus. It was daylight then, and I watched the openness around me gradually solidify. At the time I was in no frame of mind to look at what was above me. Had I looked up, I would have seen ancient stones and bricks at the top of several passageways, all put there by the prisoners who built Sing Sing nearly two centuries ago. Before that, I would have seen the peaks of the small private houses lining the road leading to the great wall.

What I would not have seen was a crystal clear, starlit night. The star patterns kept changing as the ambulance turned in different directions. Tall trees with all their leaves, and traffic signals (with three lights now), kept competing for my attention.

Suddenly, a full moon came into view. Mirona, you know the window in my cell is angled toward the north, so I had not seen the moon against a dark sky in more than five decades. It was absolutely wonderful, and I took a moment to embrace the Infinite Transcendence.

Both Oswaldo Maldonado and Lamont Davis made the trip with me. Lamont normally works days, and I would have been accompanied by Oswaldo and Anthony DiCaprio. But Lamont made a special request to travel with me even though it meant he would be doing nearly a triple shift. The way he put it, "I don't want you getting all crazy first time you seen a tree."

You and I have talked about Lamont many times. He has always had a finely tuned sense of humor. Over the years he has evolved into a kind and thoughtful man and someone I have long considered a friend.

With Arthur's passing a few months ago, Lamont remains the only other living person who has ever read any of your letters, and he was very grateful for your permission. As you know, the few he read made a difference in his life and that of his oldest son, DeShawn.

Lamont was sitting in a chair next to me when I awoke early this morning. Mirona, I am in a private hospital room. Imagine that. It has a view looking toward what I think is the west, which means the Hudson River should be just on the other side of the grassy hill in front of me. Lamont watched me staring out the window and finally said he needed to go check on something. He cuffed my left hand to the bed railing (this is procedure) and was gone for about ten minutes. When he came back, he said my workup for the program would not begin until tomorrow. That meant we had today free. And then he said, "How would y'all like to see what's on the other side of that hill?" I just smiled. Then he said he would be back in two hours. If I needed to go to the bathroom, someone at the nurse's station, just ten feet from my room, had the key to my cuffs. All I had to do was push the buzzer near my bed.

Then he left. Mirona, he left the door to my room open. The number on it tells me I am in room 418. There are no bars and I am alone. Occasionally, as doctors and nurses walk by, they do more than just glance at me. It is completely understandable. How often do they have a handcuffed prisoner as a patient?

A little while ago a tall male orderly came in with my breakfast. He seemed a bit nervous as he set up the tray that swings over my bed. I asked him if I could use the bathroom before I ate. (I have a private bathroom as well.) He stared at me for a few seconds and then said, "Wait here." As he did, we both looked at the handcuffs holding me to the railing and we chuckled. He got the key, I did my business, and he stayed in my room as I ate my breakfast. At one point, the orderly (his name badge said William) left my room for, maybe, five minutes. Now I was in a private hospital room with an open door, by myself, with no handcuffs, just eating. The breakfast was indistinguishable from the type I eat in prison every day. The thought of it all made me chuckle.

It is nearly time for Lamont to return. I have no classes to prepare and no papers to correct, so I will continue writing this after we go up the hill.

***

Oh, Mirona. The beauty. The joy. The hopefulness. I don't even know where to begin. Let me just tell it as it happened.

At about 10:30 a.m., Lamont came into my room with a wheelchair and a shopping bag. The wheelchair, again, is required procedure. In the bag was a change of civilian clothing. Lamont bought me an orange T-shirt with a picture of the basketball player, LeBron James, beneath a black Nike logo, and a pair of bright red warm-up pants with the word Adidas in large white letters running the length of the left leg. They were my first civilian clothes in a very long time. Lamont just looked at me and grinned. Then he said, "Ra-hou (he does not pronounce the L), you try and run on me, they gonna find you real fast." We laughed.

I sat in the wheelchair and he rolled me out of the building. Now I could see we were in a hospital complex. But there were still trees and flowers everywhere and, in one direction, thick woods beginning just beyond the buildings. We were going in the opposite direction, toward the hill. Actually, it was a series of undulating hills, and the crest was some distance away.

The hospital complex was well paved. However, the path leading away from the complex and up the hill was in disrepair. It would be fine for walking but not for rolling a patient in a wheelchair. I offered to walk, but Lamont would hear nothing of it. He insisted on pushing me in the wheelchair until the lack of paving and the steepness of the path made it impossible. We stopped and I stood up, expecting to make the remainder of the journey very slowly on foot.

What Lamont did next amazed me. He set the brakes on the wheelchair, then picked me up like a child and carried me what must have been fifty yards. Mirona, I weigh considerably less than I used to, but Lamont is a sixty-year-old man and weighs a bit more than he should.

At the end of the fifty yards he set me down, pointed a finger and said, "No runnin.'" All I could do was smile. Then he walked back down the hill, retrieved the wheelchair, and returned. He must have repeated this process three or four times, until we reached the crest of the hill. At the very top was an old wooden bench. He sat me there as he made his final wheelchair retrieval.

Mirona, I cannot begin to describe how beautiful the Hudson River is from what must have been three hundred feet above. I was at its widest point, just north of the Tappan Zee Bridge. To my left, looking south, I could see the skyline of Manhattan in the distance. The new 1 World Trade Center was easy to spot. As you know, I was granted internet privileges some years ago as part of my teaching activities, and I watched it being built online. The angling of its different facades really does reflect the sunlight in amazing ways.

I could only imagine seeing the building where you live. An article in the New York Times a few years back mentioned you lived in a penthouse apartment on Riverside Drive. I've viewed several of the nicer buildings there from above, on Google Earth, just to get a sense of how the Hudson might look to you. I hope you see it much as I saw it today.

A bit closer in the foreground was the George Washington Bridge. It was hard to make out the precise shape from that distance, but I could easily see the flashing red and white beacon light on top of the east tower. Remember?

I looked to my right, up the Hudson River, and I could not see Sing Sing, even though it is right on the river and much closer to where I was sitting than New York City. A large outcropping blocked my view.

At that moment I felt myself going into meditation. Before I could fully embrace it, I heard Lamont say, "Hey." He pulled a New York Mets baseball cap from his back pocket, handed it to me, and said, "You ain't been out in the sun for a while ... even if y'all don' look it." We laughed again. I thanked him and put the cap on. Lamont walked off and sat down in the grass. Then I meditated.

I anticipated a literal meditation, something that would play off of the visual images I'd just processed. Of course, we can never fully anticipate our meditations. That is what makes meditation such a joy and such a frequent source of revelation.

I meditated on one of the few events during my days as a Diablo that I have never told you about. It is strange that I never have, especially because it is one of the most important events of my life and yours.

By mid-1958, my drug use had reached its height or, more accurately, its depth. I had effectively shut your mother out despite her best efforts to get through to me. It was rare that I slept at 64th Street. Instead, I spent most of my time doing the things needed to ensure my next hit, including a range of petty crimes and sleeping in crash pads with people I would rarely see more than once.

I am sure my mother was relieved to have me out of the house. We had never had what you would call a good relationship, not in Puerto Rico and certainly not here. When I first began seeing your mother in San Juan, she insisted I spend more time with my mother simply because it was the right thing to do. I wanted to please your mother and did as she asked. Had I not been in contact with my mother during those last two years in Puerto Rico, I would have never come to America and so many things would have been so very different. I am so thankful things worked out the way they did.

One day that June, word got to me through various channels that my mother was very upset and needed to see me. As unusual and urgent as the request sounded, I felt ambivalent about seeing her. Then, unex-

pectedly, I recalled this image of her and me sitting on the airplane together as we were flying to New York City. The Infinite Transcendence was giving me just enough strength and direction. How wonderful.

My mother told me she saw Teresa storming out of her parents' building on 64th Street carrying a suitcase. Suddenly, she stopped and called my mother a "perra odiosa," which translates as "hateful bitch." Then, she said, Teresa ran across the street and into Lydia's building.

If I had been thinking clearly, I would have questioned her story and tried to get more details. In the state I was in, I simply allowed her elevated emotions to infect my own. Fifteen minutes later I was pounding on Lydia's apartment door.

It had been weeks since we had last seen each other, and yet your mother was still so happy to see me. What she did not know was my mental state had deteriorated significantly. Now this alleged insult to my mother's honor was focusing a large part of my unbridled anger, and I was intent on righting a perceived wrong.

Beyond this, I was carrying a pilfered copy of Modern Detective Stories magazine that had a picture of your mother in a negligee on the cover. Thinking back, it was a very beautiful and enticing photo. For some reason I had shown it to my mother. Her reaction was to call your mother a "putita," and that had only worsened my emotional state.

As she began to recognize my condition, your mother's joy quickly changed to concern. She tried to reason with me and explained that she had directed her words to some woman who was standing next to my mother at the time. As Lydia explained to me some years later, that woman deserved to be called considerably worse. My mother's English was very poor, and the Spanish insult was the only thing she understood. The other woman convinced her she was its intended target, just to get even with Teresa.

I refused to accept Teresa's explanation. Cutting her off, I flung the magazine at her and shouted, "How much they pay you for this?" When it became clear she wasn't going to give me the satisfaction of an answer, I screamed "Huh?" at the top of my lungs. I remember, I screamed so loudly it hurt my throat.

We both stood there, frozen. Then your mother began to chuckle in a very strange and wounded way and started to tear up. As twisted as my emotions were at the time, I remember feeling concerned by her unusual behavior. Suddenly, she was laughing and saying things Teresa would never ordinarily say.

She asked me if I wanted her to be my whore again. Then she lifted her top over her bra, held up her breasts, and asked if all I wanted was some of this, like all her other men. It was so bizarre and unexpected I found myself backing away from her. I actually said, "Are you crazy?" Imagine me saying that to your mother then.

Teresa just stared at me, smiled, and finally said, "Oh, you want to be my shrink? You want to save me?" Then her expression turned angry and defiant. She began shaking her breasts and shouted, "Maybe this will save you!"

Something in my mind snapped. I slapped her face with all my might and screamed, "Putita."

Then we just stood there. Even in my deteriorated state I knew I had crossed some kind of boundary. The realization was not just sobering. It brought me to a place of clarity that made the drugs in my system a momentary irrelevancy. (Let's call it an energetic intervention.)

I remember staring at my hand, the one that had just slapped her, and suddenly feeling horrified. Then I reconnected with her eyes. They were furious. A large, bright welt was forming on her left cheek. Both of her hands were clenched into fists.

Then the words just came out of me with an intensity I could have never anticipated: "Teresa, perdóname" (forgive me). I can remember the feeling of the words on my lips even as I write this. All the while I was staring into her eyes.

And then they began to soften. A moment later she was smiling the most beautiful smile I can ever remember and telling me she loved me. Imagine that, Mirona. Not two minutes after I had assaulted her, your mother was forgiving me and telling me she loved me.

Suddenly I had this intense urge to protect her. Teresa began talking about making a life together, as if the life I was living could just be erased; as if—imagine this—it could be energetically cleansed. Neither of us would have understood what that meant at the time. But in a refined, focused way, the Loving Oneness was actually enabling it at that very moment.

I kept trying to tell her I wasn't ready. That I had done too many awful things. That she could never possibly love what I had allowed myself to become.

But she did. Mirona, she truly did. And, gradually, her love gave me the courage and the strength to liberate the love I had always had for her.

We made love that afternoon and well into that night. It was more than passion. It was a statement of intent elevated by a sense of profound purpose.

And there was boundless hope. So much hope, Mirona. It not only protected us from the ugliness that surrounded us. It transcended the moment and embraced a future time where its resolution was both apparent and lovingly anticipated.

That is how you were conceived, my sweetheart. In love and hope and caring. In a timeless moment of infinite potential. How could I do anything less than everything in my power to help you realize that potential? I am so blessed and honored to have you as my daughter and to have in the deepest part of my knowing the image of what is already within your grasp.

My meditation lasted a little more than an hour. I spent more than half of it focused on your present image. How beautiful you are.

Rolling my wheelchair down the hill was much simpler for Lamont. My workup begins at 6 a.m. tomorrow morning, so I think I will try to get some sleep now.

I love you, Mirona. I love you so very, very much. I will write to you again tomorrow, although I still don't know exactly when, but I will. I promise.

Love and Kisses,

Daddy

***

Ed. Note:

I've tried on several occasions to begin my commentary on RL19087. It's not that I feel paralyzed. There are just so many thoughts and feelings, and I keep tripping over them. I finally told Gina, and she suggested I insert the transcript of my father's YouTube video instead.

It was recorded on the afternoon of December 4, 2016, four days before he died from stomach cancer. He still wrote me a letter that evening and even joked about his baldness. Sometime during the night of the 6th, he slipped into a coma. Early on the morning of the 7th, he was transferred to the prison infirmary. A worker who had known Raul for years placed a sheet of three-hole paper and a pencil on his chest.

On the morning of December 8, they found him almost exactly as they had left him the night before. The pencil was in his right hand. His left hand was holding the paper over his heart. He had written three lines as he lay in a prone position, obviously without seeing what he was writing. The handwriting made his early letters look sophisticated: "Dear Mirona—Always Love And Kisses—Daddy."

I plan to keep the link up indefinitely: www.raulvideo.com.

31

Transcript Of My Father's Video Message

(RVIDEO-12042016)

Raul (smiling face of a 77-year-old, thin, bald Latino man with glasses, mild accent): Hello, sweetheart. It's me. I felt pretty good today, so I thought this would be a good time to make the video.

By the time you see this … if everything goes the way we planned … (chuckles, counts on fingers). Blake gave you two envelopes, Lydia called your mother and … we'll be getting together pretty soon. If you call Lydia now, I think she'll give you all the letters. Maybe you can … (thoughtful chuckle, coughs) you can read some of them … anyway … before we get together.

(smiling pause) I know. Why didn't he call? Why did my father wait until it was too late? (conspiratorially) Mirona! Remember what we always said. It's *not* too late. (soft chuckle) It's *never* too late!

Now it's *your* turn. You get to pass along the good things that were passed on to you. (flipping gesture) Remember? The Rule has *two* parts.

(shift) Uh ... the second envelope is for your mother. Just bring it. You'll know what to do. (pause) I know what she's gone through and I ...

(closes eyes, pauses) Sweetheart, I have always loved her ... (eyes open) and I know she has always loved you. And me. Always. (smiling, head shaking, pause) And ... Mirona ... (eyes close, head continues shaking, trancelike) I love you, I love you, I love you, I love you ... (eyes open, smile broadens, gesturing intensely) I love you ... I ... *love* ... *you!* (two hand-to-lips kisses, long smiling gaze, screen goes black)

***

Ed. Note:

Aunt Lydia was aware of how sick my father was, but was still under strict orders to tell me nothing. On December 12, four days after Raul died, she received a manila envelope and several large boxes from Sing Sing. The boxes contained all fifty-plus, three-ring binders with all his letters. The manila envelope contained three white business envelopes, one for Aunt Lydia and the other two for me.

All these materials had been sent much quicker than the possessions of a deceased prisoner would normally go out. Raul's guards were aware of what he was planning and had provided the additional money and logistics to move things forward as quickly as possible.

The letter to Aunt Lydia included a series of instructions. Raul expected to be buried in the current potter's field, Hart Island, but then wanted me to have him disinterred and reburied in a proper cemetery. The necessary paperwork had also been started by his guards.

Before she did anything else or had any communication with my mother or me about Raul's death, Aunt Lydia was to secretly invite Blake to her house and give her as much firsthand knowledge about Raul and my mother—and herself—as she possibly could. At that point, Blake had never met Aunt Lydia. I myself hadn't seen Aunt Lydia since the time my mother visited my father in prison, although I occasionally answered the phone and said hello when she called Mom in Chicago.

When Blake understood her roots a little better, Aunt Lydia was to give her the two envelopes for me. The first contained the YouTube link. The second contained the crucifix my mother had given my father in San Juan the day of her graduation party.

Blake got home very late that evening, far later than I expected her, and I started right in with my usual bitching. She'd gotten her hair dyed and spiked since the last time I'd seen her, and I thought she looked like a little freak. Of course, I let her know about it, but she didn't respond with her usual defensive belligerence. In fact, she was perfectly calm and absolutely silent. I stopped halfway though my rant and just stared at her. Then she smiled, handed me the two envelopes, and quietly walked to her bedroom.

Five minutes later I was hearing my father's voice for the first time.

Aunt Lydia called me at home the next evening [Blake had given her my private number] and told me about my father's request for reburial. Three days later the boxes containing my father's letters arrived at my apartment. Each box had FedEx labels covering any evidence of its Sing Sing origins. I spent that entire night browsing through the contents. It was one of the most emotional nights of my life.

The next morning I called my assistant at home and told her I'd be in late that afternoon. I also instructed her to have one of our document conversion companies send a van to my residence immediately.

I stood there in their warehouse as eleven technicians dropped everything else and converted every page of my father's letters to digital documents, applying the numbering sequence I'd created the night before. When they were done, they handed me a thumb drive with all the letters. I followed their truck back to my building, watched them place the boxes with the binders in my study, and then went to the office.

The earliest we could retrieve my father's body and then rebury him in Gate of Heaven Cemetery [per his request] would be on January 16. The invite list according to Raul's instructions was to include Aunt Lydia, Blake, Mom, and myself. I hadn't met Gina yet. That wouldn't happen until the following Christmas.

All this was being planned without contacting my mother. I felt uncomfortable about that, but even more uncomfortable at the thought of seeing her again. The last time we'd been face to face was at a Corporate Social Responsibility Conference at the New York Hyatt back in May of 2000. This was another one of those things boards thought I should be attending, and the board at Morgan Stanley was no different. Mom had learned I'd be there and had purposely kept her name off the agenda until the last minute, assuming [correctly] I would have bailed if I'd known she was a panelist as well.

She approached me after one of the sessions and once again tried to talk about family. Once again, I blew her off. That was the atmosphere as the burial date approached.

Aunt Lydia recorded this amazing description of what happened to all of us at the gravesite. I asked her for permission to include it in the book, but she absolutely refused. Instead she insisted I let Blake tell the story.

When I mentioned this to Gina, she just laughed. Then, softly, with that amazing smile of hers: "Who else!"

32

BLAKE'S PERFECT CODA

(BGRAVESITE-01162017)

I was there when Aunty Lyd recorded what happened at Grandpa's burial, and she described it all perfectly, so I'm not sure why she wants me to tell the whole story again. It's not that I mind telling it. It was absolutely the most beautiful thing that's ever happened to me. It's just that there was so much and I don't want to leave anything out.

I was in my junior year at Columbia when I got a call from some woman with an outrageous Nuyorican accent. She spent the first five seconds shouting, "Don' hang up, don' hang up!" When I finally promised I wouldn't, she started rattling off all these amazing details about my "forbidden family"—names I'd never known, events I'd never even heard about. And I knew she was telling me the truth. The next thing I knew, I was promising to meet her at her place in the Bronx.

I used to go to the Bronx a lot during high school, mostly in my junior and senior year when I was boarding at Lycée Bonnaisse in Bedford Hills. My friend Monique would call one of her father's drivers, and depending on his Saturday morning schedule, he'd either drop us off at the Number 4 train terminal in Woodlawn or, if he wasn't too freaked, he'd drive us to where we scored our drugs. Besides their normal function, the drugs took the edge off going home on Saturday afternoon and hearing my parents fight on the phone about who was supposed to own me until Sunday night (or more often than not by then, who was getting stuck with the little fuckup).

Mom couldn't figure out how Aunty Lyd got my number. She got my cell phone number from none other than Grandma, who got the number from Daddy. I didn't know it at the time, but Daddy had been in touch with Grandma practically since I was born. They'd never met, but he tracked her down at the Chicago Housing Authority after Mom let it slip that Grandma worked there one day while she and Daddy were fighting about every-thing else. Daddy said he reached out to Grandma when he was feeling very low, just after he stopped drinking the first time and a good two years before he got visitation rights. He missed me, and he knew he'd have to get back in touch with Mom if he ever wanted to see me again. He also knew Mom wasn't talking to Grandma, but she was his only possible connection to me. Somehow he found the courage to contact her. It's so cool how these things work out.

The week before I heard from Aunty Lyd, I had my hair spiked. Nine spikes, straight up, all about six inches long. The shafts were neon pink with red tips. It looked pretty good, but it didn't quite go with the ultra-gloss black lipstick I was wearing then.

Two days later I got it all redone—turquoise shafts with cobalt blue tips. (The lipstick looked *so* much better now!) I knew there'd be massive quantities of shit flung when Mom saw me, and I'm not sure whether I dreaded it or relished it. Probably a little of both. That's where my head was(n't) then.

There were no afternoon classes that day, so I agreed to meet Aunty Lyd at her place at 1:00. To be honest, I hardly ever attended any of my afternoon classes. As a creative writing major with a famous parent who was also a generous alumnus, I had a whole bunch of wiggle room.

Living on campus gave me even more room. Mom's condo was only four blocks from my dorm, but she'd been going through another of her extended "phases" lately and it was a lot safer for us to stay in neutral corners.

The trip to Aunty Lyd's was going to be easy; the Number 6 train to Castle Hill Avenue and then a four-block walk. I'd never taken the 6 all the way up to the Bronx. It comes out of the tunnel after Hunts Point Avenue and stays above ground the rest of the way. I've always had this thing about taking new subway rides. I love standing in the front car and just looking out the window. They say it's a guy thing, but I could never figure out why.

By the time we hit Morrison Avenue on the viaduct, I was the only whitish girl on the train. I'd casually look over my shoulder every once in a while just to see if my hair was still working. I'd do that then. No one seemed to be noticing.

We were held at the Morrison Avenue station for something like five minutes for no reason. There wasn't a single announcement. Then, finally, even though the lights ahead of us were all green, we just barely began to move forward.

And then something really weird happened. As we finally pulled into the Saint Lawrence Avenue station, I began recognizing all kinds of things. I knew where the staircases would be on the platform. I knew what buildings would be visible from the front of the station, and they were there. As the train started to move again, I knew exactly what stores would be visible on the street below us. Even what color their neon signs would be. And it was all there.

In the middle of all this, I suddenly had this intense image of the east tower of the George Washington Bridge, driving underneath it on the West Side Highway the way the limo would go when I used to go back to Bedford Hills on Sunday nights. Somehow the image fit with everything else.

The feelings and this extra—I don't know—dimension got even stronger when we hit the Parkchester station. Then when the train finally got to Castle Hill Avenue, I just turned around, walked out of the car, walked back to the second staircase, walked down to street level, made a 180, walked to the corner, made a left, and then walked two more blocks. Then I turned onto Ellis Avenue and walked two more blocks. I knew every inch of where I was and where I was going. It was all happening in soft focus, like an easy high.

The next thing I remember was standing at the front door of the third house in a set of row houses. I reached out and put my hand on Aunty Lyd's doorknob.

Then, suddenly, everything just came into supersharp focus. The feeling of everything being familiar got yanked away. I looked at the number on the door and I knew I was where I was supposed to be, but now it wasn't like I'd been there before.

Then Aunty Lyd was standing in the doorway. I'd never seen her in my life, but she smiled at me like I was her oldest friend. Her first words were, "Good to see ya again!" She gave me this monster hug and let me in.

She took me right into her living room and said, "Look aroun'!" It's not that the things in there were actually familiar, but they were just so comfortable. She had this massive collection of stuff from when she used to live on West 64th Street: stacks of newspapers, bags of cat's eye marbles, half a candy store. But nothing seemed excessive or out of place.

There was a death certificate in Spanish for Inez Cruz, her mom. My Spanish isn't as good as my French, but I could make out the cause of death was *sobredosis de drogas*, a drug overdose. She told me what really happened later that night. I swear, no miniseries could've come up with a more outrageous story line.

What I was focusing on most was the photos. There had to be hundreds of them in all these little piles. Just as I was about to start on pile two, Aunty Lyd walked back in, handed me a Corona Light, and said, "We look a' dose latuh."

Her kitchen had this ancient dinette set from the fifties, straight out of some retro diner. In fact, it looked like pretty much everything in there was from the fifties, but it didn't feel trashy; just, again, so incredibly comfortable.

There had to be something like 50 of these 3-ring binders. Two were on the table. The rest were stacked on the floor or piled up on the kitchen countertop. Each one was completely stuffed with loose-leaf paper and they all had a year handwritten on the spine.

We sat down on opposite sides of the table. Aunty Lyd lit up a Lucky Strike, slapped both hands on the Formica, made this big smiling gesture, and said, "Dis is who you are!" I started smiling too. In fact, I felt so unbelievably happy I must've been smiling my ass off. Then she said, "OK. Go ahead. Ask!"

But before I could, she said, "Wait!" and held up this small black-and-white photo with a scalloped edge. It was a picture of a guy sitting on a stoop and a girl standing over him but looking right at the camera. It took a second to register. Then I just kept repeating, "Holy shit, holy shit!" Aunty Lyd started to giggle.

The girl in the picture was my twin. And it wasn't just her face. It was her height and the way she turned her head and how she held her body. I knew this person, and I knew she was super-pissed at something. I finally managed to ask, "What'd he do to her?" And Aunty Lyd just cracked up.

I told her, when Mom was normal-pissed at me she might say something like, "You're just like your fucking father!" But when she was super-pissed, she'd say, "You're just like your grandmother!" It was never "fucking" grandmother. I don't think she could put those two words together. But she didn't have to.

I had no idea what being like my grandmother meant or why it drove my mother up a wall. I'd never even met my grandmother. Now at least I understood why we were lumped into the same category. But why did she hate us?

"She don' *hate* you! She jus' afrai' you don' *love'r!*" I must've been drooling by then. Aunty Lyd took another crack at it: "She never really *met* huh mothuh. Same like you." Then she smiled. "You startin' to see de *lights* now! I *know!*"

That *really* got the conversation going. We talked nonstop until about 9:00. She told me about Mom and Grandma and Grandpa and what happened in Puerto Rico, and on and on. She even told me things about me I'd never told anybody else.

The really cool thing was she never accused anyone of anything or judged anyone. She just made the connections between everything and showed how it all ended up with the two of us sitting at her dinette table that night, bullshitting and tossing back Corona Lights. I never felt so much a part of something in my entire life.

(Mom said she was going to write the story about the three envelopes and Grandpa's video, so I'll leave that part out.)

That night I slept at Mom's condo. The next day was a workday, and Mom's driver always called from downstairs at exactly 7:30. If I happened to be there, I'd stay in my room until I heard her heels clicking down the main hallway and then the sound of the door shutting in the distance. That was my signal to crank up some Grateful Dead.

That morning, after hearing her wake-up sounds, I got dressed and met her in the kitchen. She was sitting in the breakfast nook just staring out the south windows with her black coffee. On the rare occasions when I met Mom like that, we'd get right down to some unfinished business: something I'd done or not done that pissed her off. I could always feel it before she said it.

I felt something very different that morning. It had the same intensity, but it wasn't directed at me. When I knew it was safe, I just said, "Good morning." The words sounded unnatural. Something that simple, that normal, was something I never said to my mother. She looked at me like she was trying to recognize me. Then she said, "Wait a minute," walked all the way to her study and came back with a folded piece of three-hole loose-leaf paper. It was the link to Grandpa's video. I watched it after she left. God, I cried so much.

During the three weeks before the funeral I attended all my classes and spent most of my nights at the condo. Mom and I didn't speak all that much, but there wasn't a single fight either.

One morning she called me from work and said she was having a hard time tracking down a limousine company that had one of those old flower cars, the type they used in *The Godfather* at Don Corleone's funeral. She wondered if I could help her find one.

My first class that day was at 11:00. Before 10:00, I was talking to a company in Pennsylvania that rented vintage cars mostly to film companies. They had a mint-condition 1958 Eureka Cadillac Flower Car, but it would have to be transported by flatbed to and from New York City, and it wouldn't be cheap. I called Mom and she said, "Fine, order it." No haggling. No second-guessing. I felt really good about that. Then she asked me to handle the flowers.

It's amazing how many flowers it takes to fill the open bed of a 1958 Eureka Cadillac Flower Car. The florist Mom uses had never done this before, so we had to figure out what kind of flowers would work and how high to pile them to make it look right. I downloaded *The Godfather* again to see exactly what they did in the movie. Their designers went to the max and it looked totally impressive.

When we calculated what the max would cost, it was almost the cost of the Flower Car. So we worked out three different pricing options with different kinds of flowers and different quantities. When I explained it all to Mom, she just said, "Go for the best. Thanks, Beebs." She hadn't called me Beebs since I was about nine. I absolutely hated that nickname. Now, for some reason, it sounded good.

Then she asked me to handle the priest. Understand, neither of us is what you'd call a church type. In fact, I'm sure neither of us could name a local priest if our lives depended on it.

I started calling funeral homes and got the names of Catholic priests who did prayers at wakes. But when I called their churches, I got this whole list of reasons why Grandpa wasn't entitled to their services.

One of my friends suggested I check with the chaplain at Columbia. She directed me to a Catholic diocesan priest who said he'd be willing to do just the graveside service we were looking for. For six hundred dollars. Cash. Mom said to go for it. By then Grandpa was already buried on Hart Island.

Hart Island is this 100-acre island in Long Island Sound just off of City Island in the Bronx (where you catch the Hart Island ferry). The City of New York and the Department of Corrections have been using the island since the Civil War to bury unclaimed bodies, and not just those belonging to prisoners. They've used it for preemies, derelicts, indigents, and anyone who'd just been forgotten. By now there were nearly one million people buried under every square inch of the place, making it the largest public cemetery on the planet.

But the living public wasn't allowed there until just recently. Someone or some group finally convinced the City and the DOC that the forgotten dead deserved a little more dignity, and they got a project approved to locate and identify as many of the permanent residents as possible.

The day of Grandpa's funeral, the way Mom scheduled it, the hearse would be downstairs at 10:30 with the flower car behind it. Her driver would arrive at 10:35 and we'd begin the procession to City Island.

Everyone was on time (of course). The flower car looked like this over-the-top prop out of some midwinter tropical fantasy. I was decked out in full Goth splendor. Mom looked like she was ready to chair a Fortune 10 board meeting. The priest said he would meet us at the City Island dock. Grandma was flying into LaGuardia from Chicago. She was going to rent a car, pick up Aunty Lyd in the Bronx, and then meet us at the cemetery.

People on Broadway stopped dead in their tracks and just stared. A lot of Columbia students were looking around for the cameras, figuring we had to be part of some shoot. We got the same reaction from drivers on the West Side Highway, then on the Saw Mill, then on the Cross County and then on the Hutch.

I've always loved getting off at the Orchard Beach/City Island exit on the Hutchinson River Parkway. Almost instantly you're in the middle of woods and wetlands. If you were asleep and suddenly woke up, you'd never believe in a million years you were still in the Bronx.

Monique's drivers used to take us to Orchard Beach, always before or after it was officially opened for the summer. We'd get high, walk the crescent of the beach from end to end a couple of times bullshitting in French, and then sit down and watch the sunset while we got high again. I remember, you could see the City Island Bridge perfectly from the jetty at Section 13. We just never had a reason to go there.

As our procession reached the City Island Bridge, I had a sensation like the one I had on the Number 6 train, but this time it wasn't as if I'd actually been there before or knew the landmarks. There was—it's the only way I can describe it—this "shape" about the place. Everything about City Island was part of a shape I can't physically describe, but I know it's a shape. (Parts of City Island look a lot like parts of Newport, Rhode Island, but that has nothing to do with what I was experiencing.)

The hearse driver told us earlier he'd gotten directions from the Department of Corrections and that we should follow him. But he never gave us the address of the ferry pier, so we had no way of knowing exactly where we were supposed to go. When we stopped at the light at Fordham Street, I knew we had to make a left. And we did. It was in the shape.

As we made the turn, the shape changed. Now it defined the street we were on and the part of Long Island Sound that began three blocks ahead. A kind of light was glowing in different parts of it.

I remember looking at Mom and trying to figure out if she was experiencing the same things. From the concerned look on her face and—this is the really amazing thing—from the part of the shape she represented, I knew she wasn't seeing what I was seeing. It was right there, right in the shape.

The priest I hired was standing on the last patch of solid ground before the dock. We said hello and I handed him the envelope with the cash. He politely asked that we drop him off at the Mount Kisco Metro-North station after the burial.

The Hart Island ferry was tied up at the far end of the dock. A man with a NYC Department of Corrections jacket signaled Mom and me to board. The priest had already been told he wouldn't be making the crossing.

There were four young Black guys and several armed guards already on board the ferry. The guys were lashing down twenty-one narrow pine boxes piled three high. The boxes glowed with different intensities, and I knew immediately there were bodies in them. I also knew two of them had surrendered their life forces just a few hours earlier.

At that point the man with the jacket took us aside and explained what was in the boxes. He said the four young men were Riker's Island inmates who'd earned the right to do burial detail and that we'd be the first civilians in memory to accompany an exhumed body back from the island. Then he just smiled at us.

Hart Island was straight ahead, I'm guessing less than a mile from the dock. As soon as the ferry pulled out, the shape began to change again. Now it was so intricate and glowing in so many different places I could barely take it all in.

For a second I had an image of the inside of Grandpa's casket. Mom had ordered it, and like everything else, it was super high-end. At this point it was waiting inside the hearse back at the dock, empty. Grandpa's instructions to Aunty Lyd were that he'd have no wake and that no one should open his pine box, so the plan was to have the pallbearers simply lower the box with him in it into the gutted innards of the casket. Somehow in my image this had already happened, and it was stunningly beautiful.

The crossing couldn't have taken more than five minutes. Three official-looking men in suits and ties were at the Hart Island dock standing almost at attention around a single pine box. They introduced themselves. Two of them were the warden and deputy warden of Sing Sing. The third man was the commissioner of the New York State Department of Corrections. They were very gracious and drove Mom and me in an old van on a quick tour of all these dilapidated, mismatched buildings scattered around the island. We were told the entire place was now run by the Department of Corrections and that at one time or another over the past one hundred and sixty years the buildings had housed a Union prison camp, a women's insane asylum, a tubercularium, a yellow fever quarantine site, a boys' reformatory, and even a secret Nike missile base during the Cold War.

When we got back to the dock, the pine boxes we'd traveled with had been removed from the ferry. They'd all been replaced by the single box holding Grandpa. It still had a few clumps of dirt sticking to it. The four inmates were standing on the dock in front of the boxes they'd transported, just staring at that single narrow box lashed to the ferry's deck. I'm sure they'd never seen a prisoner—much less a dead and buried prisoner—given that much respect.

The two wardens, the commissioner, Mom and me all got back on the ferry. I could only focus on Grandpa's pine box. It had this amazingly simple shape that just sparkled. I'm not sure why, but I walked up to it and extended both my hands over the place where I knew his heart was. Then I knelt down and rested my hands on the same spot. It felt incredibly beautiful, and I think I was smiling.

When I looked up, Mom was standing over me and staring with this confused look. I asked her to join me in my knowing. It took a few seconds. Then she genuflected, touched the box with one hand, came out with this muffled, shuddering sob, instantly snapped back up and moved away. I stayed on my knees with my hands on the box the entire crossing.

At the City Island dock, all six pallbearers were standing outside the hearse. Our three vehicles had been turned in the opposite direction. The casket was sitting outside on a dolly. Four of the pallbearers came on board, lifted Grandpa's box, and carried it off. It seemed very light. The two other pallbearers opened both halves of the casket lid and the first four slowly lowered the box in. It fit with plenty of room to spare.

Then we were on our way. Just before we reached the City Island Bridge, I had to turn and look. Right behind us at funeral procession distance was a car driven by the deputy warden. The warden was sitting next to him and the commissioner was in the back seat. I wasn't sure, but I thought they were being followed by two other cars.

The priest was sitting across from us on the rear-facing seat. He was dead quiet and made very little eye contact with either Mom or me, but spent an inordinate amount of time studying this little piece of paper stuck in his prayer book. At one point while we were still on City Island I looked over at Mom and realized she was just staring straight ahead, blindly. I'd seen my mother in pretty much every kind of emotional state, but I'd never felt her scared like this.

We continued north on the Hutch and exited onto the helix that leads to the Cross County Parkway. While we were on it, I looked back again. Now there had to be at least eight cars behind the deputy warden's, all with their headlights on. The last car was flashing his four-ways. I said nothing to Mom.

We exited the Cross County and headed north on the Bronx River Parkway. I was still focused on my Grandpa shape and all the illumination. Then, suddenly, it all got pulled away just like on the way to Aunty Lyd's and I was aware of this pulsating fear. It was coming from my mother, and I felt it spilling all over me. Literally. I must have gasped. We locked onto each other's eyes and a heartbeat later she broke contact.

By the time our procession entered the cemetery, the tension in the car was unbearable. Mom's eyes were darting all over the place. She finally fixated on something in the distance just as I turned to check out our procession. There were no cars behind us.

We stopped. Grandma and Aunty Lyd were standing in the roadway next to a rented white Chevy just a few feet ahead of the hearse. I remember trying to match her with the picture I'd seen and what I might become. She was very attractive and elegant looking, with short, swept-back gray hair, a lot like the way she wore it in the picture. She could've just come from some photo shoot.

About twenty yards off the path, parallel with the hearse, there was this mound of dirt covered with blankets of fake grass. Next to the mound was an open grave with several wooden planks across its mouth.

The pallbearers exited the hearse and did this nicely choreographed thing with the casket, finally setting it down on the planks. Then they opened our doors. For the first time we were in the same space as Grandma and Aunty Lyd.

Mom and Grandma just zoned in on each other. It wasn't so much a staring contest as a million questions. It's like they were talking two different languages and desperately listening for common words and phrases.

Mom must have gotten—or not gotten—some message. She broke eye contact with Grandma and started marching toward the grave on her own. Grandma followed, and then me. Then Grandma suddenly turned back and she and I began our own very emotional conversation. The difference was, we were speaking the same language, although Grandma was still learning it. Aunty Lyd stood off to the side like she knew something was coming.

Then Mom looked back and realized there was something going on between me and Grandma. I thought she was going to accuse me of something, but her fear suddenly began asking questions about her mother. I tried to answer.

Then Grandma jumped back in. It was like a three-way conference call. Most of what we were saying started with words like "why" or "why couldn't we" or "what did you mean by." Sentences got piled on top of sentences. Then whole paragraphs. Then entire volumes. Bigger and bigger pieces kept getting overwritten.

By the time we got to the grave, we'd given up on attempted thought-words and were just putting out pure emotions. Grandma moved to one side, Mom and me to the other. Then Mom looked directly into the grave through this open space between two of the planks and I felt this sharp jolt as her fear shot off the scale.

While all this was happening, the priest was adjusting a thin purple stole around his neck. He glanced at us and must have figured it was as good a time as any to start.

"In the name of the Father and of the Son and of the Holy Spirit. Amen. Oh Lord, we ask that Thou looketh with mercy upon Thy son …"

He hesitated and just stared-eth at that same piece of paper in his book. Finally, he mumbled an almost incomprehensible "*Ray*-yule …"

That was the Rosetta Stone. It took all the babbling and emotion and boiled it down to this perfect singularity. Almost in unison we shouted back, "*Raul!*"

The man just stood there, frozen. Then he backed up a few steps.

Suddenly we rediscovered speech. I heard myself crying out, "Grandma! Grandma!" and then I felt my legs running toward her. She was crying, "Blake! Blake!" We met up at the foot of the grave, crying our eyes out and hugging like we'd just discovered how. Mom started crying, "Ma! Ma!" Seconds later we were in a three-way embrace.

Then Aunty Lyd piled on. She threw this quick head-tick toward Grandpa's coffin and smirked, "Fuckin' genius, eh?"

Three of us started to laugh, and finally Mom too. The priest backed up a few more steps.

It took a while for us to release one another. Then there was silence, but not the kind from a few minutes earlier. Now we knew where all the points were that supported each one of us. Grandma asked silent permission and we granted it. She looked at Grandpa's casket, smiled, and began to whisper, "*Raul, Raul* …" Then she knelt down on the first plank covering the grave, rested both her hands and her cheek on the foot of his casket, and began to cry very softly as she repeated his name.

One by one we joined her around the casket. Mom was crying, "Daddy, Daddy." Aunty Lyd called him *Raulito*. I cried for my Grandpa.

When our mourning period was over, we smiled at each other again. Grandma turned inward and approached some kind of barrier. When she got past it, she slipped her hand into her coat pocket and slowly produced the crucifix Grandpa gave her the day of her high school graduation party. As she held it up, it started to glow.

Then, just as Grandma began to lay the crucifix on the casket, Mom started to laugh again. She reached into her own coat pocket, pulled out the second envelope I had given her, and handed it to Grandma. The image of a cross was practically embossed on it.

Grandma opened the envelope and took out the crucifix she had given Grandpa that same day. She held it up with the other crucifix and began to laugh and cry. We all joined her. Then both crosses began to glow, and as the glow got brighter, they slowly began to intertwine.

We stood up and another shape described Mom, me, Grandma, Aunty Lyd, the crosses, and the casket. Everything was glowing and the light said "*Pass it on.*" I looked at Aunty Lyd and I knew she was seeing and knowing the exact same things. Then I looked at Grandma. She wasn't seeing what we were seeing, but I sensed she was right on the edge of knowing it.

Grandma kissed both crosses with the most delicate kisses. Then she looked at Mom and smiled the same kiss to her. Her smile also asked Aunty Lyd and me for a little assistance.

I started lifting the back of Mom's hair. She was surprised, but she let me do it. I knew Mom wasn't seeing or knowing, but she was in this place not too far from both, and I tried to tell her she could feel good about it.

By now Grandma was placing her cross around Mom's neck. Aunty Lyd attached the clasp. Mom was going into this limp, sobbing trance. Grandma gave her a huge embrace, then gently lifted Mom's right hand and placed it over the cross. Mom started taking short, shallow breaths. Her eyes asked me, "Why do I feel this way?" I smiled back, "Because you're supposed to. And it's all good."

Suddenly Grandma needed my eyes. I offered them, but then I couldn't help toggling between her eyes and the second cross.

I was in this place in her knowing. When she knew it, she smiled and put Grandpa's cross around my neck. Aunty Lyd went to lift my hair, but quickly realized it doesn't work that way with turquoise spikes. Mom even attached the clasp. Then Grandma gave me this massive hug just like the one she gave Mom. I started laughing and crying and clutching the cross with both hands. The light began to glow much brighter and the shape began to change again. Most of the light was coming from Grandpa's coffin, and the shape took in most of the cemetery around us.

For the first time I was aware of groups of men standing at least half a football field away from us in all directions. There had to be almost a hundred of them. Some like the wardens and the commissioner were dressed in suits and ties, but most were dressed in simple winter clothes. They were mostly Black or Latino, and most of them were old. A few of them were hugging and you could tell a lot were crying. Still, just about everyone was smiling.

A second later we all got it. Grandma finally spoke the words: "Class reunion." We chuckled.

Then it started. The shape changed again, and Grandpa's coffin began to glow with this superbrilliant light. It shot upward and merged with a light coming from—I don't know—infinity. The light split, and a massive shaft covered the four of us. I was gasping and laughing. Aunty Lyd was shrugging and chuckling like she knew this part was coming all along.

Grandma was reaching deep into her knowing and managed to touch just the edge of what was happening. Mom watched all of us with questioning eyes asking for details. She knew she was being led. For once she just trusted and followed.

Then Aunty Lyd stepped back out of the light and began to watch the three of us with this really cute smirk on her face. Oh yeah, she knew what was coming.

Two *triangles* of light rose through the lid of Grandpa's coffin. They followed up the beam, and where it branched off toward us, they turned and descended. One of the triangles stopped crotch high, and its points made contact with the three of us. The other triangle stopped chest high, and its points connected directly to our hearts.

My arms reached out to Mom and Grandma. Instead of grabbing my hands, they both moved in closer, reached out, and touched my shoulders so that our arms formed a third triangle.

The space between the three triangles filled with even more light. It was so bright it was all I could see. Mom and Grandma were both trying to see it through my eyes.

After about a minute, the light and the shape began to fade very slowly. Before it left, it asked to be remembered. Grandpa absolutely promised me we would meet.

Then the three of us were just standing there, hands on shoulders. The smiles returned and a moment later the embraces. Aunty Lyd was part of our group again. There were still no words, just this beautiful afterglow warmth.

Then the applause began. At first it was just a few distant men. Then whoops and hollers, like they'd just watched a Hail Mary pass get caught in the end zone with no time on the clock. It turned into a total celebration. I felt myself joining in, and I could feel a few of the men who fully understood it in their knowing. Everyone shared this boundless hope.

Aunty Lyd didn't need an invitation for whoopin' and hollerin'. Grandma joined in, right up to the edge of her upbringing.

Mom was still confused and amazed and smiling and tearing up. Suddenly she turned to Grandma and grabbed her hand. Her thoughts were outpacing her words.

"Ma, when … How did he know? … When you … When you said … Why didn't you? …"

She must have gone on for fifteen seconds, just like a little kid. Grandma's smile just kept growing. Finally: "Just let me … I know … as soon as … just … I promise … everything … I *promise* you … *Ev*erything!" Then Mom began crying her eyes out and hugging Grandma like there'd never been a time she didn't.

As we walked back to the cars, the men slowly began walking toward Grandpa's casket. Mom marched ahead of us and instructed the pallbearers to unbunch all the Flower Car flowers and lay them next to Grandpa. They hopped to it.

The priest was inside Mom's limo. He looked like he'd been there for a while. No one remembered him leaving us. Mom instructed her driver to take him wherever he wanted to go—*now*.

The four of us got into Grandma's rental. By now the men were forming a single line right behind this growing pile of flowers. The first man picked up a few, walked onto the first plank, stood for a few silent moments and gently rested the flowers on Grandpa's casket. Then he turned and gave a respectful nod in our direction.

After watching the next man do the same thing, Grandma exited the car and stood at graceful attention. The rest of us joined her. We began to return the nods.

The ritual went on for almost an hour. After the last nods were exchanged, the four of us got back into the car and Aunty Lyd broke the spell.

"I don' know 'bout *you* … but I'm fuckin' *starved!*" We cracked up. It was my turn. "I know this great Thai restaurant in Irvington. Sambal. We can be there in twenty minutes. Go back to the entrance and make a left." I was only sorry Grandpa couldn't join us.

We took an upstairs table at a window that looked out onto the deck and the Hudson River. The sunset was gorgeous. The food was great. The drinks and the conversation were endless. It was less about revelations than making sure all the old walls were demolished. Mom was exceedingly kind to the waiter who got stuck closing at 2 a.m.

Over the next few days I spent a lot of time swapping energy notes with Aunty Lyd. She told me it was best if I stayed in the dorm and let Mom sort things out on her own. That's how Mom always has to do things.

Grandma decided to stay in New York City for an extra week, and I spent a lot of time with her as well. Three days after the funeral she took me to this high-end day spa on the Upper East Side where we got the full treatment. I'd never been to one of those places in my life, and it was wonderful. We walked out with almost identical makeup and hairstyles. People were staring at us on the street.

I learned a lot more about her that week. She'd retired from her job as chief operating officer at the Chicago Housing Authority about fifteen years earlier, not so long after the last time she'd met

Mom at some conference at the New York Hyatt. At that same conference she'd been approached by the chief operating officer of Grey Advertising, who wanted to know if she'd ever modeled. Damned *right* she had!

Grey had originally wanted her to appear in a series of Hispanic Senior commercials and print ads. But when they saw her portfolio with all the high-fashion shots Miron had taken (and never used), they decided to launch her as an Hispanic Senior, an Anglo Senior, and a High-Fashion Teenager all at the same time.

Grey used several of her 1958 high-fashion shots for a Piaget campaign. Miron had posed her with these moody gestures and matching expressions against shadowy lighting and flowing drapery. She wore a series of high-end gowns that looked even more dramatic in this kind of textured black and white. All the shots were drop-dead gorgeous. Three of them were enlarged to one hundred feet and mounted successively on the north face of the Times Square Tower. At the foot of each shot the agency superimposed a Piaget watch and the words "Timeless Class." The blown-up pictures and a few others were used in a series of magazine runs. I didn't remember seeing any of them. Then again, I was six at the time. Mom told me she was very aware of them.

Grandma kept a couple of her high-fashion shots on her cell phone. After she returned to Chicago, she emailed me a bunch more. Then one night, about three months later, we went through a few hundred of her modeling shots at the new condo she'd just moved into in Soho. She'd kept them all.

Besides the high-fashion shots, there were binders full of art and other commercial shots Grandma had done for different magazines and catalogues. There were stills of several recent Spanish TV commercials she'd done for Tide and Blue Cross. She did six (hot!) covers for a pulp fiction magazine called *Modern Detective Stories* and even a few faceless bullet bra shots for a 1958 Sears Catalogue.

After I'd oohed and aahed my way through all of them, she went into a closet and took out an exquisite black gown. It was one of those form-fitting Balenciagas she said were all the rage in the late fifties. It was the first dress she'd worn for her first high-fashion shoot, and it was still in mint condition.

Grandma had this outrageous idea. I would wear the original black Balenciaga and she would wear another original in beige she'd found online. She was only, maybe, two pounds heavier than me, and you just knew she'd still look spectacular in either dress.

We made reservations at Balthazar's on Spring Street for 9:30 on a Saturday night in late June. I wore this classic pair of black pump heels. Hers were identical but in flaming red. We both wore vintage Ray-Ban sunglasses.

The place was packed with the hippest of hipsters but, so help me, there was this air-sucking gasp as we walked in. Unimpressable Soho types couldn't figure out how not to stare at us. We were given one of the best tables and spent the entire evening pretending not to notice.

Every so often someone would casually approach and try to place one or both of us at some party or event. One very artsy-looking guy said he remembered me from my Piaget ads. I took off my sunglasses, smiled, and asked, "You mean the ones from fourteen years ago?" He went instantly stupid. I waited a perfect three Grandma seconds, pointed to her, and said, "I believe that was *Teresa's* shoot." I think I heard his brains explode.

As we prepared to leave, our waiter explained there were still nine rounds backed up for us. Grandma asked him to offer our sincerest gratitude to whomever.

I'm not a girly-girl type. I know I have good looks (now I know where I got them) and there's never been a lack of people hitting on me. I've slept with exactly three guys my entire life. The second one was a mistake and hardly counted as sex. The idea of doing girly dress-up, much less with my grandmother, and parading it through one of the hottest restaurants in Soho is something I could never even imagine. But I did it and I loved every second of it. Grandma didn't have to imagine a thing.

Outside, a couple of paparazzi started flashing cameras in our faces. My first reaction was to block them with my hand. Grandma touched my arm, struck the perfect pose, and gave me a tiny nod. My pose followed. After a few more shots, she elegantly removed her sunglasses and there was a whole new round of flashes. Finally one of them asked, "Who are you?" Grandma offered another perfect three-second smile: "I'm *Teresa*. And this is Blake." We glided off.

Grandma bought us several more matching outfits. My favorite was the tailored black leather pants with the sequined tops. We'd show up at different hot spots every now and then and usually get the same reactions.

Gradually—and especially after *People* Magazine ran an entirely wrong piece about who we were—Grandma began offering the paparazzi more information. At first she limited it to being a former chief operating officer who was out with her granddaughter. (She'd already made me a semi-celebrity at Columbia.) Then she began to tell Grandpa's story.

Finally one evening she told some reporter about our energetic experiences and how Grandpa figured into them. That got a lot of press. It was just before Christmas of 2017, and now reporters were approaching me on campus. I wasn't sure what to tell them.

One of them asked if my experiences were like what Doctor Gina Gilford talked about on her television show. I knew about *Energy With Doctor Gina,* but I wasn't a big television watcher.

That same night Aunty Lyd called me and said we'd all been invited to Christmas dinner at Aunt Gina's country house in Somers. I think *my* brains exploded. Aunty Lyd and Aunt Gina had been in very close contact for the last few months. Actually, they'd been in contact for decades, but lately they'd been talking a lot more about Grandpa. Mom had made thumb-drive copies of Grandpa's letters and given one to each of us. Aunty Lyd's wound up with Aunt Gina. She started going through his letters and realized he'd developed a far more refined version of her own Energy Medicine model long before she'd ever thought about creating one. She wanted to begin incorporating his teachings and practices into her practice, but felt she needed Mom's blessing before she could start. She got that blessing on Christmas Day.

When I was introduced to Aunt Gina, she looked at me with her Energy eyes. Then she smiled from ear to ear and gave me a huge hug. Yeah, we both knew.

That day I also met Matthew, my future boss. He was there with Lisa, this absolutely beautiful Chinese-American girl and one of the kindest people I've ever met. They were both segment producers for Aunt Gina's show. Matthew and I had a long talk about the show and our energetic experiences. Before we left that day, Aunt Gina asked me if I'd be interested in going through the show's intern program as soon as I graduated from Columbia. With Matthew as my mentor. That meant I'd be working at one of the top syndicated shows in the country for a guy who was just two years older than me and who understood everything I'd experienced at Grandpa's burial. (Did I mention he was *tres* cute?)

The first project I worked on was a segment on archetypes that tracked against a lot of what Joseph Campbell had written in *The Power Of Myth*. Matthew had started the project while he was an intern but got sidetracked. He handed the entire thing over to me and told me to just go for it. I did (with his constant guidance, of course). The segment got positive reviews, and Matthew and I have worked on all kinds of other segments since then. I swear, he's a genius.

One night, just after Christmas 2017, I was over at Grandma's new place. We were bundled up on the terrace sipping our Proseccos and watching Soho sashay by when she said she had something she wanted to show me.

We went inside, and she brought out this beautiful leather binder. It contained nothing but full-color nude shots Miron had taken of her when she was eighteen. They weren't the trashy, selfie sexting shots clueless fifteen-year-olds post online. These were drop-dead classy.

She was lying on or standing in front of this white silk sheet with different colored lights shining on it from different angles. Miron had placed two fans outside the frame that kept the sheet bubbling around her, so parts of it were always out of focus. The effect was beautiful.

Grandma used a single prop, a red silk sheet, and wore a pair of red pumps (which I recognized immediately). The red sheet was always strategically draped and the effect was incredible. She was a tease, a temptress, the ultimate vixen, but that internalized smile said she was always in control. She never begged or pandered. She just shared what was hers to share.

I kept gasping. Grandma kept chuckling. It was like looking at myself in the bathroom mirror: her butt, her boobs, where her waistline cut in. We were body doubles except for one thing—her nipples were a pale pink.

I asked Grandma for the shoes and a second later for the red sheet. (I knew she'd still have it.) Then I went into her bathroom and worked on my hair and makeup. She had this gorgeous white silk robe behind the door and I slipped it on. Then I stepped into the red pumps which, of course, fit perfectly.

And then, I don't know why, I just vamped my way into the living room trailing the sheet behind me. My heart was pounding. Grandma was laughing and applauding. I tried to duplicate her expression from the photos.

Finally I let the robe fall off my shoulders and just stood there, naked and feeling incredibly beautiful, a tribute to the woman who'd done it so much better fifty years earlier. Now it was her turn to gasp. I began positioning myself and the sheet the way she did. Grandma kept telling me how gorgeous I was.

Then I stopped posing and pointed to my nipples. They're an unusually dark brown, almost like a burnt umber, and never seemed to go with the rest of my coloring.

She smiled and began tearing up: "Like your grandfather's."

We both started to cry. Grandma stood up, wrapped the sheet around the two of us, and embraced me like a little child.

Aunty Lyd and Grandma are my two best friends. Aunt Gina's a friend as well, but she's also my boss's boss and my DEM (Doctor of Energy Medicine). We all get each other, we all like each other, and there isn't a conversation the four of us can't have.

Mom's another story. Within a month of the funeral she informed Morgan Stanley she was going to break her employment contract and several other contracts. At first they tried the stickless carrot approach and promised she'd be next in line for CEO. When Mom demanded they put it in writing, things went south. There were threats of subpoenas and lawsuits and countersuits. All sorts of vicious things were written about her in the press.

Mom, of course, knew exactly what she was doing as well as where all the skeletons were hidden. Once the dust had settled, she presented a written list of demands to the board and got them all approved in less than twenty-four hours. They wound up paying her not only the full severance she would've been owed if they'd fired her but a much larger additional lump sum, plus seven years of consulting fees. And her stock options. Both sides agreed to a very long-term nondisclosure agreement.

We'd stopped fighting, but it wasn't like we were really that much closer. She seemed to accept that I was very close to Grandma, Aunty Lyd, and Aunt Gina. I always had this sense that Mom saw closeness as weakness and something people could exploit. Still, as things settled down after the funeral, she seemed to be accepting (if not fully trusting) the closeness of the people around her. It doesn't sound like much, but for her it was major.

Right after that Christmas dinner, Aunt Gina began discussing Grandpa's writings on the show and the impact they were having on her Energy Medicine model. It was just a matter of time before she asked the object of those letters to do a guest appearance.

Mom was really hesitant about doing *Energy With Doctor Gina* the first time. Throughout her entire career the media had always talked about the last glass ceiling she'd shattered or the next brilliant financial strategy she'd crafted (or, more recently, the things she'd supposedly gotten away with).

This would be a very different Roni Pod, one with a resurrected first name, an adopted last name, and a mission totally divorced from her financial life. We all knew she was absolutely sincere about promoting Grandpa's message and memory. The question was whether the public could accept her at face value even as she was having problems accepting what it all meant on a personal level. I don't think she expected people to take sides about her as passionately as they have. None of us did. Then again, everyone seems so much more frightened and passionate about everything these days.

Like most people on this planet, Mom doesn't have an expressed gift, and that means she needs a guide. To be honest, even people with expressed gifts need a guide. But without the ability to see the Energy, there has to be a level of trust established with that guide until the energetic cleansing process starts to produce concrete changes.

I was really surprised when Mom said she was going to start seeing Aunt Gina professionally. Then again, there was nothing left for her to do short of ignoring everything that had happened to all of us at the burial and all the letters Grandpa had written to her. Someone had to guide her through it all.

But the absolute last thing I expected was for Mom to write a book about who she really was and how she really felt. For her, that's taken more than just incredible guts. It's taken a level of trust in all of us I didn't think she could ever muster. It's amazing what Aunt Gina can help people do and become and overcome through Energy Medicine. My one goal in life is to learn how to do what she does.

People tell me they have a hard time trusting or believing in Energy or spirituality. What I tell them is, it has nothing to do with trusting or believing. That'd be like saying I don't believe in radio because the waves are invisible and I don't believe in things I can't see, and therefore I can't trust the sounds I'm hearing. Energy is just what we are and what we're all a part of. It's just there. Spirituality is just a word that describes the way Energy works with people. There's no faith or belief involved. It's just what is.

Which is why—and Aunt Gina drives this home at staff meetings all the time—our mission is *not* to preach a counter-gospel of Energy or Energy Medicine. Those of us with expressed gifts have the responsibility to live lives that reflect the positive nature of those gifts and their capacity to engender hope. None of that comes automatically. Because Energy is so natural and so pervasive, there's always the option of ignoring it (or, as I've seen on more than one occasion, misusing it). We also have a responsibility to compassionately forgive ourselves, honor our pasts, and perfect our own lives as best we can even as we continue to resolve our relationships with our ancestors and others.

Mom, I know, gets the responsibility part as well or better than most people with expressed gifts. But she reaches this tipping point every time Aunt Gina's energetic cleansings hit a certain depth in her soul. It's the point where you have to just let it go because you can already feel it going. Mom can't. That's when she begins hanging onto her fears for dear life. Which means she has to surrender the chance of discovering real hope, at least for the moment. I know she completely gets what she's doing on an intellectual level, but that can't make it any easier. Most people in her position would probably blame Energy Medicine or claim it was a hoax and just go on doing whatever it was they were doing.

Mom doesn't have that option. No, I take that back. Mom won't allow herself that option. She's made a commitment to Grandpa and Aunt Gina and to all of us, and she's not going to renege.

One day a few weeks back while we were having breakfast, Mom began looking at me with that intense look she has. Two years ago we would've been ten seconds from a major fight.

Finally she said, "Why didn't he just write them to you?" And she kept looking at me. There was nothing for me to say. Then she looked out the windows: "Because he wanted me to …"

She cut herself off and just kept looking. It was the first time in a very long time that I knew, in the deepest part of my knowing, that I loved her. I really, truly loved her.

— *Blake Palmer*

PART II

33

BELATED GREETINGS FROM MUMBAI

Mumbai, Maharashtra state, March 24, 2024 (2 AJ)

Ed. Note

This is the third or fourth time I've tried to write whatever it is I'm still supposed to write. I know it's been at least a year since the last time I tried.

There's not a lot making it in these days. The messages that do get through, especially the ones from North America, are using the AJ designation pretty consistently. I'm not an AJer, but if people want to see another senseless act of violence as the fulfillment of some prophecy, who am I to disagree?

If they'd bother reading their own books, they might notice what didn't happen. No final battles, no galloping horsemen, no wheels within wheels, no seven seals, no rapture. Just bloody rubble and enough dirty bomb contamination to keep what's left of Jerusalem evacuated for a few more years.

According to them, we now live in the time After Jerusalem. Two years after. Actually, it's one year, six months, and a few days since 9/11/22. Christianity never seemed concerned about the months and days once Anno Domini became all the rage, but I'm not sure the same will be true for people intent on marking their lives from a moment of destruction. I'm surprised they haven't come up with a dating system that's precise down to the hour. Or the second. So they won't feel cheated out of a single, officially designated opportunity to take justified offense and promise justified retaliation. Imagine what they have to look forward to in another month, or a year? Or twenty years?

I think most AJers are still trying to convince themselves the Apocalypse actually happened. Or is happening. Because if it didn't or isn't, if the holiest sites for Jews, Christians, and Muslims simply ceased to exist outside of some profound scriptural context, if one cell of enraged fanatics could evaporate the sacred symbols of half of the planet in a single afternoon without somebody's God Almighty showing up to wreak personal vengeance, then ... what? Do the atheists get to say, "I told you so?" Do the Hindus and Buddhists go on a marketing blitz? What?

In the beginning, we all thought the retaliation was going to be instantaneous and unending. I'm sure that's what the Nihilists were banking on as well. No one expected a two-month lull, as if *the entire planet had gone into catatonic shock and then mourning. With the tangible symbols that supported all that good and all that bad instantly gone, the sudden vacuum knocked the planet on its collective ass. I think we needed time to change the planetary baseline, to lower our collective threshold of hopelessness to something akin to Europe in the Dark Ages before people could translate their fear and emptiness into rage and start acting it out in earnest.*

I suppose I should be thankful we're all· alive. It's hard to imagine what it must have been like in New York City in the weeks and months after the Lincoln Center riot. The three of us must have been (and probably still are) near the top of several hit lists. If it hadn't been for the Foundation for Change, I'm convinced we'd all be just so much fodder in another Central Park mass grave.

Since [amazingly] I've gotten past more than a couple of paragraphs this time, I think I'll keep going. With social media gone and all the server and database corruption, who knows how many people will ever learn our part of the story. It's important for me to write it and then try to upload it any way I can.

The Foundation for Change is based here, about 80 kilometers outside of Mumbai. It was started in 1999 by a then-New-Delhi-based Hindu pundit named Atul Arora. While everyone else was worrying about Y2K, Baba-ji, as we fondly call him, was encouraging people to embrace the incipient changes he was detecting in the core energetic frequency of the planet. His read was that the changes would be good and that they'd have a positive world-wide influence that would last for decades, if not centuries.

A lot of very smart and influential people began to get Baba-ji. And it wasn't just because of what he was saying. The man has gifts that would have amazed even Gina.

Actually, come to think of it, they did. Baba-ji was very aware of what Gina was doing with her show and had reached out to her a couple of months before she was murdered. He left her an open invitation to not only become a member of the foundation board but to live here at foundation headquarters. Gina was surprised and honored by the offer, and immediately sensed she wasn't its actual object but rather a designated mechanism of retransmission. She explained all this to Matthew and instructed him to tell no one else. I assume she thought most of the people around her would've been frightened by the implications. Of course, she was right.

Three days after her death, Matthew reached out to the foundation. He was told Baba-ji was now extending the invitation to him, Mom, Aunt Lydia, Blake, and me. Matthew and I were both tapped for board membership as well. If we were interested, we should all get in touch with Grete Pedersen.

The entire world had seen Grete's Benetton "Change" ads by then, and all the "Change" websites that carried her picture. But she'd dropped out of sight. What we didn't know at that time was that she and her fiancé, Sonny [Sanjay Mehta], were being held at Kandahar air base by a U.S. general who would soon find himself dead at the hands of one of his own bodyguards. Grete and Sonny managed to escape, and within hours were appearing on Christiane Amanpour's first [and only] worldwide broadcast.

We and most of the planet watched Grete's beautiful, bruised face issue a call for peace. Then we watched most of her family get murdered right before our eyes.

Matthew called Christiane's show the next morning [the phones and the internet were all still working] and explained who we were. Within twenty-four hours, we were on a private jet with Grete and Sonny headed for Mumbai. I say "we." Aunt Lydia flat-out refused to leave. ["No fuckin' way dey gonna make me leave dis house!"] Mom and I had transferred as much of our money as the new banking rules allowed. We'd all packed as much of our lives as each of us could fit into two suitcases. Thumb drives of everything imaginable were created at top speed, including the book.

Then we were gone. And obviously not a day too soon.

The first few weeks were hectic. Much of our time was spent monitoring what was happening in different parts of the world. I remember being impressed by the scope of Baba-ji's information network.

One afternoon, two former U.S. presidents [at this point, there are nothing but former U.S. presidents] showed up at the foundation. I had this lovely chat with Bill Clinton. We managed to identify three different occasions when we'd almost met. I was glad to hear Hillary, Chelsea, her husband and her children were safe and doing well. Sadly, the same couldn't be said for all other former presidential families.

Things like this kept our minds occupied. Then Jerusalem. Then, as nations began to fracture into factions, it became increasingly difficult to monitor all the players, then key players, then whoever had launched an attack on whomever that week, then that day.

Soon, factions and players were springing up, combining, acting out, and dying off faster than any of us could keep up with. A depressing reality was sweeping over us, and Baba-ji was spending much of his time reminding us it would all end in a good way. The Infinite Transcendence had declared it to be so.

I'd been here about a month when it hit me that I'd never have breakfast in my condo again or stand on the west terrace and look out over the Hudson River in every season. It's not that where we are isn't beautiful. The foundation is situated on what must be twenty acres of gently rolling hills. Parts of the property are beau-tifully manicured. There's this incredible grove of banyan trees, and there's never a time you can't pick some exotic fruit from some exotic tree and not be delighted by your first bite. The weather's always warm or verging on hot, but there's always a soft breeze.

The foundation building itself is somewhere between an embarrassingly large house and a moderate-sized suburban office building. As you enter the foyer, there's a series of exquisite Indian sculptures all lit with museum-quality lighting. Classical

Indian rags are usually playing through the speaker system. There's a Michelin-class kitchen, an executive-level dining hall, and sleeping accommodations for about a dozen.

The office wing has—or had—the best computer and communications setup I've ever seen, plus some equipment I've never seen before. The technical, support, and domestic staff for the whole facility numbers fourteen people, and they still do a splendid job. They have their own dormitory building about fifty yards from the main building.

So I guess there are far worse ways to live.

But, of course, it isn't home and never will be. Then again, what is home? Baba-ji still loves to sucker me into that conversation. In the end he points to Mom, Blake, and Matthew, and asks, "Now, where is home?" Then he chuckles. Always that delighted, delightful chuckle. I can't help chuckling back. Even now. Morgan Stanley would be shocked and mortified.

Blake was very upset David was being left behind. She called him just after we heard back from Grete and cried her heart out. Then, not long after we got here, she told me her father wasn't supposed to be with us, not because of what he'd done or not done but because of what the Infinite Transcendence was facilitating. I was amazed at the way she said this, not like some terrible sentence had been pronounced but with an openness and acceptance I'd never seen in her before. She still trains with Baba-ji several times a week and, I swear, she reminds me more of Gina every day.

She and Matthew have continued the kind of collaboration they began on Gina's show. Not long after we arrived, they began working on the outline of a screenplay about Lydia's life [working title: "Lydia"]. Then Blake did an outline of a screenplay about our family [working title: "Dear Mirona"], and then they worked on the outline of one about Matthew's family [working title: "Heritage"], all within the first six months we were here. At that point they switched over to producing an online, information/inspiration, daily-then-weekly webcast until our server network was hacked and rendered essentially inoperative.

Baba-ji takes a read on Aunt Lydia every few days. As of two days ago, he says her Soul is still united with her body and her energy signature is very strong. Matthew hasn't said anything, but I don't think his mother is doing well at Gina's old house back in Somers. I was surprised when he agreed to come here without her, but it was obvious, even in the beginning, he and Blake were far more than business associates.

The truth is, Blake told me a while back she and Matt were deeply in love. Not that you couldn't see it, but imagine. "Gordona" [my secret nickname through several companies—think Michael Douglas in "Wall Street"] has actually produced a child capable of knowing deep love for another human being. Really, how cool is that?

My mother is amazing. She's still giving Spanish lessons to the foundation staff [and me]. And she's the first one to check on our crops in the morning.

I should explain. While there are still a few fresh vegetable sources in our area, there's far less in the way of prepared foods. So we're evolving into a complete farm-to-table enterprise. The problem is, so is Mumbai, a city of more than 21 million people. Some Nihilist sect set off a series of simultaneous bombs about fourteen months ago that knocked out about a third of our regional food processing and packaging facilities. Most of them were back online within two or three months, but the downtime created shortages and lag times that have never really been corrected.

Add to that last month's sarin gas attack on the dhal processing facility [by whomever], and people are beginning to leave the city just to be closer to sources of food in the fields. Their numbers aren't critical [yet], but if the present trend continues, we could begin having real problems in the next six months or so.

I bring this up to Baba-ji every so often just to say it to someone else. He chuckles, hugs me, and says, "You are building such a wonderful future!" And for the moment, at least, I stop worrying about it.

I've tried to finish the book several times. It's still missing the epilogue Gina told me I had to write. When I mentioned this to Baba-ji the first time, he just looked at me wide-eyed. Then a smile spread across his face and he started laughing like a Santa. All he kept saying was, "Yes! Oh, yes! Of course!"

Over the past three years I've reread the last draft Gina reviewed on multiple occasions as well as all the emails she and

I exchanged during that period. The last time I read everything was easily a year ago. If she were here now and saw how much I've written today, I know what she'd say: "Now read it all again. And this time, listen to your voice, Mirona."

I'll do that, Gina.

34

Just *BRILLIANT!*

Mumbai, Maharashtra state, March 25, 2024

Ed. Note.

*O*h, Gina! My brilliant, BRILLIANT Gina!

"Listen to your voice," she said. The problem is, I was always too busy calculating what I should write to actually listen to what I'd written.

I've always had a gift for crafting memos that could eviscerate some person or position but leave me totally protected. I could do the same thing with legal documentation. Our lawyers used to go crazy when I'd edit their briefs and affidavits without their permission. In the end they'd leave in every change because they knew I'd thought it all out three steps beyond anything they could calculate and had anticipated exactly how the message would be read and how the other side would react.

Old habits die hard. When I was rereading my preface yesterday I became aware of all these little buffers I'd inserted in just the right places. They distanced me—but just barely—from endorsing what my father was saying. The preface was the last thing I wrote [not counting my notes after Gina's death], and I was actually creating a blanket disclaimer for everything I'd written before that. It's just something I would do.

If you read the whole thing quickly enough, you'd think I believed what my father had said about Universal Energy. But the only thing I personally committed to in the preface was promoting "the knowledge" of his writings because they seemed to have more practical potential than any other essential writings I'd come across. That's it. No personal testament. No unqualified assumption of liability. Just a nonbinding commitment. Yeah, there were all these little hints of personal sentiment, but they were all located close enough to words like "Gina says" or "Gina believes" to give me cover.

I never really listened to myself, right through the last of my countless [edits] yesterday evening. If I had, I would've realized it wasn't just Raul who was changing his voice—it was me, too! Sure, I might've been using my adult filters to parse the legal effect of my words but, on the inside, the person writing was the same child, teenager, or adult Raul was speaking to. We really were having a conversation. It's just that my part of it was being documented a bit later.

Early this morning, once I got all this into my thick skull, I started listening to my father's voice very carefully. And then I started thinking about the letters I'd chosen to comment on. I'd reduced the number to ten—ten out of thousands. After Gina hinted at the need for a shorter book, I dutifully edited out most of his brilliant descriptions of energetic functionality and Energy Medicine methodologies and focused on just the personal stories because they were the ones that pushed all my buttons. Just like Daddy and Gina knew they would.

And I called what I was writing "commentaries." So very distant and professional sounding! But they were really just the evidence of the explosions his letters were triggering in my Soul. Of course, my baffles and filters were always scanning for opportunities to dilute or cull out anything that could've been read as an unqualified embrace of my father's inspiration. But my filters couldn't hide the fact that I was doing battle with the darkest parts of me in a very public way, precisely as I was supposed to, so everyone could see. Including me! Finally!

It was amazing to reread the commentaries from Mom, Blake, Gina, and Aunt Lydia. Especially from Aunt Lydia. None of them were fighting battles at the time they were writing. My father's words seem to have inspired a clarity in their voices, a certainty about what they'd experienced on an energetic level. Aunt Lydia took it all to an extreme, insisting that nothing or as little as possible come between her voice and the evidence of her voice on the printed page. She knew in the core of her being that what came from her Soul had integrity, and she didn't want that integrity sullied in the slightest by subtlety or nuance. It all had to be right there, right up front. It was the only way she knew to make sure I got it. Or as much of it as I was going to get then.

I remember thinking their commentaries were giving me cover. They were saying the things about Raul I refused to say or was simply too afraid to say. I was pushing off against them and my father, just like I used to push off against anyone or anything I felt confronted by, except this time I was doing it with my father's blessing. Instead of getting into a fight or getting myself pregnant, I was shining this massive spotlight on the before and, possibly, the after of my life just like he knew I would. And he had to know I'd eventually see what I'd illuminated.

Here's what it's all about:

HOPE!

That's all it is. Every word my father ever wrote was about transitioning—CHANGING—from lives of fear and hopelessness to lives of hope. Recognizing our common Energy and the methodologies of Energy Medicine are probably the best way to achieve a state of universal hopefulness, but they're not ends in themselves. I didn't get it back then. If more people had come to that same realization four years ago, I might not be writing this in exile from such a beautiful prison.

Oh, fuck! That's it! The book finally has a name! How could I have missed it? Brilliant, Daddy, just BRILLIANT!!

And now I know exactly what I'm supposed to write—no, what I want to write—in the epilogue. You and Gina both know too, don't you? I'll write it tomorrow morning. It won't take long. Then Mom and me will have the whole day to ourselves to talk about it while our loving young couples, Beebs and Matt and Gret and Sonny, are on their nature walk with Baba-ji. Imagine! In the middle of all this!

HOW ABSOLUTELY FUCKING HOPEFUL!!!

35

Editor's Epilogue

Mumbai, March 26, 2024

"You <u>may</u> <u>not</u> pass along the <u>hurtful</u> things that were passed on to you. You <u>must</u> pass along the <u>good</u> things that were passed on to you."

—Raul Guzman

***

Dear Mom,

I *love* you! … *so* much!… for everything you are and for everything you've given me without ever naming your price. Thank you for never giving up on us and for always, somehow, *hoping*!

Love and Kisses,

Roni

***

Dear Beebs,

I _love_ you! … _so_ much!… for seeing past the things I couldn't see past and, after that, for helping me know they weren't really me in the first place! Thank you for giving genetics such an incredibly good name!

Love and Kisses,

Mom

***

Dear Aunt Lydia,

Goddamnit! I _love_! your dirty jokes. No one's ever made me laugh so hard so many times and no one else ever will! I promise!

Love and Kisses,

Mirona

***

Dear Gina,

There are no words. Or at least no words are necessary. And if they are, you already know them and you know they're coming straight from my heart this time.

Love and Kisses,

Mirona

***

Dear *DEAREST* Daddy!,

Oh, Daddy! Daddy, I *love*! you!

I! ***love***!! you!!

I!! <u>LOVE</u>!!! you!!

I LO

PART III

36

○

POSTSCRIPT

Date: 23 July 2041

Global Archives Reference: 26.MNA.B4071

Description: Bound printed book, 527 pages, 25 cm. by 17 cm. by 3 cm., missing front hard cover and first four and one-half interior pages, including all identification of authorship. Contains three individual stories designated "Dear Mirona," "Lydia," and "Heritage," sharing common characters and events. An example of wartime domestic drama and one of the earliest and most informed literary accounts of energetic intervention facilitated by Energy Medicine modalities. Attributed to Blake Palmer and, possibly, Matthew Warner.

Source: Retrieved from ruins of a suburban Cleveland, MNA library, June 2028.

Background: At the time Baba-ji, Sonny, and I had just finished the first draft of the Unilistic Accords. We had managed to messenger or, in several instances, transmit copies to core Theonic groups in Northern Africa, Western Europe, Southern Asia, and Middle Northern America, and were attempting to visit as many of them as possible to get direct input. Final agreement on a Unilistic text would not occur for nearly a decade.

One of the key MNA Christian groups had relocated to the outskirts of Cleveland after the most recent food riots had subsided. We were, perhaps, two kilometers from their headquarters when we came upon a nearly intact architectural pediment lying directly in our path. It was the type associated with neoclassical structures and used extensively in civic buildings through the mid-twentieth century. We all experienced significant illumination from an area directly behind the pediment and decided to explore.

Most of what had been a library was rubble. There were some human remains, and we immediately ensured the unfulfilled transition of two individuals. We then proceeded to search for documentary or technological artifacts, but there was little that would have met current archival collection criteria, except for one thing.

Sticking out of the rubble was a small corner of a thick and nearly intact book. It was missing a front cover and a few pages but was, otherwise and unusually, almost perfectly preserved. As I held it the first time, I imaged the anger of a male and cleared it. I believe he was a participant in a book purification ritual that had been unexpectedly interrupted.

More remarkable than the condition of the book were its contents. Its three separate "Trilogy" stories were the obvious realization of ideas I had heard discussed in Mumbai in 2024, just before the Foundation for Change headquarters were destroyed.

The morning of the foundation attack, Sonny and I were off with Baba-ji, Blake Palmer, and her beloved Matthew Warner, on one of Baba-ji's nature hikes at a local farm. There was never a time before his death that he didn't take at least one a week. I knew Blake was the granddaughter of Raul Guzman. Her mother, Mirona Guzman, and her grandmother, Teresa Betancourt, were also living at the foundation at the time.

As we walked, Blake spoke in unusual detail about her experiences during Raul's burial and her connections with the book her mother had written based on a small sample of his writings. She said she always carried a drive containing Raul's writings and her mother's book, never knowing when she might find a computer connected to a functioning server network. She promised to make me a copy of the drive when we got back to the foundation.

Blake attributed everything good in her life to her mother. She and Matthew were still looking forward to writing the three screenplays they had already sketched out. They would pay tribute to their families and their life experiences and to the transformative power of Universal Energy and Energy Medicine.

Once the fires were out at the foundation, Blake was able to identify her mother's remains. Amazingly, one of her hands was still clutching an intact thumb drive containing just the final thirteen pages of text and a title page for *The Prison Dialogue.* Her grandmother's remains were never identified.

All of our computer equipment as well as all records of Blake's screenplays had been completely destroyed. Just before she and Matthew set out for Mumbai, she handed me her original drive and the one she had recovered from her mother and asked me to upload both whenever I could. That was the last time I saw or heard anything about either Blake or Matthew.

What Blake handed me that day was the last surviving complete copy of Raul Guzman's letters. (Fragments of his original letters were eventually found in the burned-out remains of Mirona Guzman's New York City residence.) Her drive materials provided the basis for continuing modification and expansion of the Energy Medicine model developed by Doctor Gina Gilford and currently being implemented globally.

The book included on the first and second drives was, of course, *The Prison Dialogue* by Blake's mother, Mirona Guzman. It was the second element designated for inclusion in the post-war Global Archives and the first book to be nanoplasted into the initial kranix/cos-con call-up following first-tier implantations. (Full cos-con network activation remains scheduled for 11 September 2044.)

To date *The Prison Dialogue* has been translated into 27 base languages and read by an estimated 1.4 billion people, nearly one-quarter of our global population. Mirona's unceasing struggles to find hope as she confronts a series of chronic negative frequencies, even as her world—our world—is collapsing around her has been a source of profound inspiration for our entire planet. For many her book has also provided a first, loving introduction to the foundational works of Raul Guzman and our Met-Holistic Infrastructure.

It remains a mystery how and when *The Trilogy* was created and then wound up as a printed book. While most forms of advanced technology, especially those with life-saving potential, were being systematically sequestered, simpler technologies, like digital printing presses, continued to play a universal and, at times, unfortunate wartime role. The question is, why would one be used to print an unknown author's first book instead of regional propaganda? And why was the book found only in suburban Cleveland? No other copy has ever been recovered. We have no conclusive answers.

I read *The Trilogy* for the first time about a month after I found it. It was and remains for me one of the most moving and inspirational books I have ever read. As engrossing as it would be as a work of pure fiction, its factual basis makes it all the more compelling. I feel *The Trilogy*, like *The Prison Dialogue*, deserves our collective attention as we strive to preserve and illuminate the best of our terrestrial human roots and accomplishments.

Disposition*:* The hard copy of *The Trilogy* is today designated an Archival Element, although I shall maintain it as a personal item. I have also today designated *The Trilogy*'s contents for level-one inclusion in the Phase 3 kranix/cos-con call-up.

Hon. Grete Pedersen, DEM Primus, Global Magister Emeritus

37

ADDENDUM

Date: 14 July 2075

On this, the 25th anniversary of the first *Pana Mondis Europa,* I have inscribed a second dedication to my great-granddaughters in the original copy of *The Trilogy*. It reads:

> *To my Anjali and Archana.*
>
> *To HOPE! First, now, and always.*
>
> *Love,*
>
> *Your Gammy Gran*

The original of *The Trilogy* is now in safekeeping with their mother, my granddaughter, Amelia. I failed to mention in my original notes of 2041 that after my initial reading of *The Trilogy* I meditated and, after congruent internalizing, inscribed a first dedication. It reads:

To Mom,

Who has given so much and is loved by so many,

All my hopes and dreams. And especially …

<u>ALL!!!</u> <u>MY!!!</u> <u>LOVE!!!</u>

(Always)

Beebs

THE END